Mind Reader

A Novel

By

Steve Godofsky

 MAYFAIR BOOK PROMOTION, INC.
PROFESSIONAL PUBLISHING SOLUTIONS

For information contact the publisher:

Mayfair Book Promotion, Inc.
P.O. Box 91
Foresthill, CA 95631

www.mayfairbooks.com
prospct1@foothill.net.

ISBN: 978-1-934588-35-2

Printed in the United States of America.
Distributed by Reality Press for Mayfair Book Promotion, Inc.

Mind Reader

Chapter One

    I've always lived in Lake Monroe, New York, so has Donny. We were born here and our parents own homes in the same neighborhood. Donny and I went to kindergarten together at the Wilburn School and we've been best friends ever since. It was the summer between our junior and senior years at Lake Monroe High when what we call the "Incident" happened. And now, many years later, I wouldn't be surprised if we're still best friends when the first one of us dies.

    Donny's folks met at college. They went to some big school out west. When they graduated, they got married and Donny's mom started work as a researcher for an employment agency in Lake Monroe because her sister knew the guy who owned it. Donny's dad went to work at a local architecture firm. He always knew he'd be an architect. While they lived in their first house in another part of Lake Monroe, Donny's dad spent much of his time working on designs for the house they eventually lived in on our street. It took them nine years but they bought the land, knocked down the old house that was on it, and built their family home according to Donny's dad's plans. It wasn't flashy or anything, just a really nice brick house with lots of rooms (including a cool rec room) and a backyard with big trees. And, of course, they had a backboard and basket that Donny's dad bolted above the garage door so Donny's friends could play hoops whenever they wanted.

    Donny's sister, Valerie, was born first. That was the year after Donny's parents (their names are Ed and Sue Morris) moved to Lake Monroe. Donny was born three years later, and so was I. In fact we were born in the same hospital about three months apart. I'm older. We didn't actually know each other until we were placed in the same kindergarten class. We pretty much liked each other from the minute we met. We became best friends before the Incident, and remained the same after it.

    Of course even though we've always been friends a lot of other things have changed. Lake Monroe did its fair share of changing over those first 17 years of our lives. My mom used to say that, when they first got there, everything was like a fairy tale. She loved living there. Honest, friendly people always looking out for each other, respecting each other and helping each other to cope with the world. No one locked his or her doors. There wasn't much crime, no gangs, a few friendly police. Everyone in town seemed to have enough money and people seemed happy. Mom says life was much simpler then. As the years went on the economy changed and grew weaker, people lost jobs, they spent more than they earned, they got angry with each other much more often, crime increased, a few street gangs moved in, and there were even signs of organized crime in the town. Mom says it's a different world now. She thinks it's colder somehow and it often makes her sad just thinking about it.

My folks moved here a few years before the Morris's came. Our house was much older and a little smaller than theirs. It had aluminum siding and no rec room but it wasn't bad. My dad sold insurance and I guess he didn't make as much money as Ed Morris, but that didn't mean a whole lot to Donny and me. We just wanted to have fun, get through school with decent enough grades to go to college, and be, well, successful I guess. I'm not really sure what successful really meant back then. I guess it was doing well in school, going to college, meeting the right woman, getting married, having children, getting a good job and having all the stuff that goes with it … you know, cool car, nice house … things like that.

Even with all of its changes I think Lake Monroe was a nice place to live. Since we were close enough to the relatively big city of Eastchester, NY we were able to go there pretty often to do more things than you usually can in a smaller town. When both Donny and I got our licenses we could drive to the city to see sporting events and concerts, go to some restaurants … you know. Donny had his mom's old car … a 5-year-old Buick. I just borrowed my mom's Toyota when she let me. It was fine.

Sometimes we drove up to Kenworth State Park. Now that was really special and only about 30 minutes away. We had some nice parks in Lake Monroe but nothing like Kenworth. They said it was about 13,000 acres of land. The park had some of the highest waterfalls on the East Coast cut out of a huge gorge, like a little smaller Grand Canyon. There were campgrounds, picnic areas, places to swim in the river and steps carved into the cliffs along the sides of the gorges that let you walk right under the waterfalls. It was really spectacular. Donny and I took girls up there for picnics because it was very cool.

Probably the only thing that was really, really bad about living in Lake

Monroe was the weather. I'm sure it still is. One year our winter started with snow … in September! Ugh. And you basically didn't really see the sidewalks again until it was almost April. 160 inches of snow! I lived there most of my life and that winter still freaks me out. That's like 13 feet of snow! I guess, to be fair, it was a pretty unusual winter that year. Most of the time we got about 70 or 80 inches of snow, but still!

As a teenager, there wasn't anything really exceptional or unusual about Donny Morris. I mean he was always a great guy, but I don't think anything about him stood out to other people at that point in his life. By high school, he was about my height (5'10") and had kind of a slight build that filled out as he got more mature. He was not exactly delicate back then but when we were growing up some people had called him skinny. In his early years he had his light brown hair cut short most of the time. But in high school he was wearing it longer and down onto his forehead. I think when girls began to matter to him it made a difference in how he presented himself. He had a little acne when we were just starting high school but he grew out of it in one year. When he was younger, Donny thought he should've been better looking than he was. It's not that he was bad looking or anything back then, just kind of average. You know … average height, average weight, brown hair, brown eyes, that kind of stuff. But girls started to think he was kind of good-looking around the time he turned 15.

His grades in school were always B's and C's except for math where he never got less than an A. He always was a decent athlete who really loved basketball, he just wasn't great at it. So when I made the Lake Monroe High School Varsity Basketball Team and Donny didn't … well, he was depressed. We'd been shooting baskets at his house since we were little kids but once I made the team he seemed to lose interest in playing ball with me anymore. I understood but I felt bad for him.

But there were things other than math that made Donny special to some of us who knew him well. Donny always had a big heart. He cared about people for no reason other than the fact that they were people. He went out of his way to help others. If he was on a team or in a group with a goal, he always did more than his fair share. Donny always went a step further. He was a giver. And there was this other thing about the way his mind worked. I think people would just call it great intuition. He had a great sense for people and situations and always seemed to know how they thought. But he just never realized how capable he was. But without confidence and self-esteem he never thought he was good enough for the popular girls - like Carla Banes.

Carla was something all right. She was one of the most popular girls in school. Partly because she came from a pretty wealthy family that gave her beautiful clothes and taught her how to always look her best. Partly because this girl had such natural beauty with long, shiny black hair that flowed more than halfway down her back; unearthly light green eyes that drew you in like magnets; and a slim, long-legged body that other girls would die for. Yeah, that was Carla -- a knockout! And partly because Carla had a quick mind and an even quicker tongue, she could cut you in half with a sentence or even a look. And she didn't hesitate to cut down people she didn't have any use for. She was just plain nasty sometimes. She even knew how to work the teachers … especially the males, not that she needed to, because she was smart and got good grades in just about every subject. Carla could flirt like her life depended on it … and you knew she loved turning it on.

The problem for Donny was that Carla didn't really know he existed. Oh, she knew who he was all right. It wasn't a big town. But she couldn't have cared less about him or most of the other guys in school. Not the case for my friend Donny though. No, he was nuts about Carla. Like a lot of the other guys Carla was his dream. A kiss and more from her was Donny's greatest fantasy, and he made himself miserable over it. In Donny's secret dreams he often pictured himself amazingly acquiring super-strength or the ability to fly like Superman and sweeping Carla off her feet with some fantastic feat of super-dom. That's how I know Donny and I were friends at a level most people never reach. He told me his fantasies with Carla -- as silly as they were. I told him I understood. I had my own fantasies of course.

You might be surprised to learn Carla and I became friendly. That's right. Actually it was because we were randomly paired as lab partners, sophomore year, in chemistry. She was kind of a snob at first but I decided I wouldn't take any of her condescending crap so I acted like I didn't care much about her. Of course that got her miffed and she started doing stuff to get my attention and approval. It was great. By the fourth week of lab we were talking about all kinds of things just like real friends do. I didn't like her viewpoint on certain things, but God was it fun to look into those eyes every day. We actually had lunch together once in awhile because chem lab was the period right before, and our classroom was right next to the cafeteria. I'll never forget the first day I introduced Carla to Donny. I felt bad for him. He had such a crush on her and she just sort of nodded and said hi. She really didn't even look at him. I was thinking, "Boy she can be a bitch can't she." But that little "hi" was a big deal for Donny. I don't even want to think about what went on in his mind when he was home alone that night.

The Petersen family had recently moved into a house about a mile away from the Morris's. Dr. Petersen worked in the Neurology department at Lake Monroe Medical Center and his wife had recently written a successful children's book. The Petersen's had three daughters: Melanie, Sarah, and Rose. Melanie and Sarah were still pretty young at the time of the Incident but Rose was our age and sat right behind Donny in home-room.

Rose was a very short girl who reminded me of that old Irish folk song "When Irish Eyes are Smiling" my mom used to hum on St. Patrick's Day. It was because Rose's eyes always looked like they were smiling or maybe even laughing. She had blond curly hair, wall-to-wall freckles, and these twinkly brown eyes that just sparkled, especially when she smiled. She was pretty tiny. My mom called her petite. She couldn't have been more than five feet tall and she had kind of a little boy's body. I've always really liked her personality. She was a good student, a gifted pianist, and a little bit shy. She also had a good sense of humor. But she mostly made fun of herself. I talked to her on her first day at our high school and she never forgot me for being friendly to her. I sort of thought of her as one of the guys. She always seemed like the kind of person you could tell anything. She liked me too. She used to ask me what I thought of things she did and she made me feel like she really cared about my opinions.

But Rose's real weakness was Donny. Yep … from pretty much the moment she met him she'd fallen for him. She was too shy to do anything about it directly but she used to tell me about her feelings and I'm sure one of the reasons was so I'd check out Donny's feelings for her. When Rose talked about Donny I was surprised by how much thought she had put into what made Donny tick. She felt the weight of his crush on Carla and, I think, even through her own feelings for him, she felt his pain at Carla's indifference to him. She knew what a kind and thoughtful person he was. She was very impressed with his math skills (they were in the same math class). But she also had a firm grasp of Donny's remarkable intuitive skills. She saw him in a number of situations with other people and noted, with admiration, how he seemed to be able to put himself into other people's shoes. And she adored him for it.

Of course Donny didn't reciprocate. No, it wasn't the same as Carla treated Donny. He liked Rose. He thought she was a good kid. Whatever that meant to Donny it certainly lacked passion. Poor Rose. Head over heels for Donny but, at that point in his life, he couldn't see or care about anyone but Carla.

Chapter Two

I liked Lake Monroe High School. It wasn't a brand new, high tech school like some of the city schools we heard about, but it had everything most kids needed to graduate with a well-rounded education and have fun doing it. Since there weren't really any slums in Lake Monroe most of the kids that went there came from decent families. Oh there were some poorer parts of town but they weren't very big and they weren't very poor.

The high school had a quality faculty. Many of the men and women who taught there had graduated from Lake Monroe themselves and chose to come back to live and teach in their hometown. The classes weren't very big so you got to know your teachers and vice versa. I think that was one of the reasons that the students from Lake Monroe always tested well on national tests, like the SAT's. We got a lot of attention.

I was a pretty happy guy in high school. In my junior year I had a B+ average, excelled in history and science and I was a good athlete. Although I didn't start, I was on the varsity basketball team and, even though I didn't have one steady girlfriend until my senior year, I was invited to many parties and went on a lot of dates. I had mostly good times in my junior year.

Until the Incident, though, life in Lake Monroe was pretty predictable. Donny and I did most things together. We played basketball (until I made the team … then we played soccer because Donny was better than me at it and he insisted). We played a lot of video games. We started a really bad garage band (I mean REALLY bad). We were both into computers and technology … computers were pretty new back then. We liked hiking and camping. And we saw a lot of movies and read a lot of books.

Of course we both liked hanging out with girls. But Donny had that bad crush on Carla. It was like a disease until the Incident.

If we didn't eat lunch in the cafeteria, most of us hung out at a place called Angelo's. We'd also go there, if we had time, after school and sometimes on weekends. Angelo's had great pizza and burgers and cool video games. It was a great place to go with your friends to meet people. Carla Banes and her friends went there a lot too.

Donny liked going to Angelo's until Carla started showing up there with Rob Talbot. Then it became painful for him. It kind of made sense that those two would find each other because Rob and Carla were mirror images of each other. Rob was a tall, good-looking guy who just happened to be one of the best running backs in New York State. He was also, as the result of a well-planned campaign of someone else's design, President of the junior class at Lake Monroe high. Rob's grades were just okay but, for as long as we knew him, he told us he was going to go to Harvard and then he would become a lawyer. No one believed him and just about everyone was sick of hearing about it. Biggest problem with Rob was he was a snob and kind of a bully. Sort of like Carla. Big surprise, huh? He really thought he was better than most of the other kids - maybe in some ways he was.

Carla and Rob looked like something out of a movie. And, of course, Donny was pretty jealous. He didn't like Rob to begin with and couldn't stand the thought of him with Carla. Actually he couldn't stand the thought of ANYONE else with Carla. It was tough because Carla and Rob were together most of the time and, sometimes, they just seemed to be everywhere that Donny and I were. We'd see them at Angelo's, or in the cafeteria, and at the movies, or in the parking lot after school. I tried to reason with Donny about the whole thing. You know, I'd tell him that even though Carla was good-looking he could find a much better girl to spend his time with. Rose told him the same thing.

Rose was one of the most real girls I had ever met. She was honest and straightforward as could be. And she cared so much for Donny she'd have done almost anything not to hurt him. So she told him that Carla wasn't worth wasting his time on and that he should look around and pick one of the many fantastic girls in Lake Monroe. Of course Rose was hoping Donny would wake up one day and realize that she would be the best match for him. But, at that moment, Donny didn't even get that Rose was crazy about him. It frustrated her terribly.

Because Donny, Rose, and I didn't have anyone special in our lives just then we started to hang out together. I mean Donny and I still did guy things but somehow I'd look around at our table at Angelo's, or in the movie theatre, or in the rec room at Donny's house, and it'd be the three of us. I guess Rose just fit in with us and we were comfortable with her. She liked guys better than girls so she didn't have a lot of girlfriends. Sometimes we'd go to a concert together, or ice-skating, or to a football game. It was pretty easy for Donny and me, but I know it was tough on Rose. She wanted to get closer to Donny. I knew it and she, of course, knew it. Donny was the only one who didn't. Of course, the Incident changed that.

Every day we sat in a booth at Angelo's and sometimes we'd have a difficult conversation that came out of Rose's desire for Donny to think of her as more than a friend.

Rose would start, "Neither of you guys has been out with a girl, other than me of course, in a long time. Don't you miss going on dates?" she would ask.

Donny would say, "You know, I'm perfectly happy with our little threesome until the right girl realizes the error of her ways and recognizes that she's with the wrong guy. I can't really see dating anyone else right now."

Rose would frown at the lame reference to Carla, and answer, "If by the right girl, you mean that bimbo over there with Rob, you need to come to your senses. The only person she'll ever love is herself." Rose rolled her eyes.

Then, in my own well-meaning way, I would usually say something like, "Guys, I think the two of YOU would be a great couple. You should explore that, forget about Carla or anybody else, and see what happens. I could be on my own pretty easily if I had to and the two of you as a couple - terrific! Think about it." I would laugh when I said this but it didn't really help to soften the moment. Right about then both of them would shoot me really uncomfortable looks and the subject would get changed. I really wanted Donny to get together with Rose. I thought the world of them both and I really thought the two of them would fit together like a hand in a glove...but I just didn't know how that could happen. Of course, after the Incident, a lot of strange things happened.

Chem lab was always kind of interesting for me because it gave me one-on-one time with Carla. She was an interesting girl. I'd often look at her and wonder if she knew what an effect her looks had on young guys. Does a beautiful girl realize the power she has? If she grows up to be a beautiful woman does she realize it then? I didn't know.

It didn't take me long to know that Carla's favorite subject was Carla. Not that it was a surprise to me but I just hadn't known many people who could be that self-impressed.

She'd walk into the lab, come over to our table and say, "Hi Evers, what's up with you today?"

I'd usually answer with something sarcastic like, "Oh, you know, Carla, I've just been waiting for you to arrive so life can begin."

"Funny, very funny." She would say.

I'd ask, "So what did you do this weekend?"

"Well, Rob and I and some friends went to this great restaurant on the lake called Bradbury's. It's very expensive."

"Oh, I'm impressed. I know about Bradbury's. I'm surprised your boyfriend sprung for the money."

"Rob spends lots of money on me. He knows I'm worth it. What did you do this weekend … play video games with the other dorks at Angelo's?" She laughed. She would sometimes get this really nasty bite to her words. It was like twisting the knife after you've inserted it.

"No, actually, Rose, Donny and I went to Viv Perry's party. You know Rose Petersen right? There were a lot of people at the party. It was fun."

"I know who she is, the little one with the face full of freckles, right? I heard the party was a snooze and no one good showed up," she replied.

"Well if good means none of the snobs showed their faces that would be right. I can't understand why you and your friends think you're so special. The school, the town, and the world all would probably do pretty well without you." I laughed.

"You know we're the most important kids in the school. We're the best looking, get the best grades, are the best athletes, the best dancers, and are definitely the coolest. It must be really boring at a party without us," she said trying to be funny. The sad thing was that inside she really believed it.

"Ugh. You are just too obnoxious. Seeing as you're so caught up in yourself, how do you even have room for Rob in there?"

"There's always room for Rob. I'm really into Rob. You know that, I've told you before. We make a fantastic couple."

I closed the conversation with, "You sure do. Like no one else could," and went on to talk about chemistry.

Like I said, Donny knew Rob Talbot … but he didn't like him. In fact he usually went out of his way to avoid him. I remember one day, though, in the school cafeteria. There was no way Donny could avoid it.

Donny was sitting with this guy Mitch Corwin, who was in his math class. Mitch had asked if Donny wanted to have lunch and since Donny had no other plans, he said yes. They got their trays and sat down when Rob walked over. It seems Rob and Mitch lived next door to each other. Mitch asked Rob if he wanted to sit down and, Donny immediately stiffened up. But Rob said yes, put his tray down next Mitch, and there was Donny, right across the table from him. Donny was uncomfortable but he had just begun eating, so he couldn't get up and leave.

"How're you doing, Mitch?" Rob asked.

Mitch said, "I'm good, Rob. We just came from math class. Oh, this is Donny...the math genius, in case you two haven't met."

Donny just nodded and Rob said, "We've met, right Donny?"

"Right," Donny said.

Mitch said, "So Rob, how come you're not with your other half, Carla?"

"She went out for lunch with some of her friends. She says we spend way too much time together. Not enough time to be with her friends," he said. "You know, it's fine with me. I mean she's terrific and everything but I can think of other things I could be doing too."

Donny couldn't help himself, "What could be better than being with Carla?"

Rob looked at him for a second and said, "Well, there are my friends for one. Football might be another. But, then it's really not any of your business is it, Donny-boy?" He mocked.

Mitch quickly said, "Easy Rob, I think Donny's just saying that Carla's pretty special. It's a compliment, right Donny?"

Donny wanted to say, "It's not really a compliment. I just can't imagine what you could do that would be better than spending time with Carla, you asshole," but he didn't. Instead he said, "She's great Rob. Most guys wouldn't want to let her out of their sight for a minute. You're a lucky guy."

Rob grunted and said, "Well I'm not most guys. But, yeah, she's great. Probably the best-looking chick in school."

Donny had enough. He listened to them talk about nothing important for another ten minutes and then excused himself.

Rob waved goodbye without even looking at Donny. Donny didn't care. He just wanted out of there.

Donny and Rose had history class together. He was good at it and Rose didn't particularly care about history. She would rather have been in almost any other class, except she got to see Donny in history.

One day, after the history teacher announced there would be a test in two days, Rose asked Donny if he could help her study. She had never done that before and she was very hesitant about doing it. All she could think about was the one-on-one time with Donny.

Donny said okay and they agreed that Rose would come over to Donny's house to study the next night. Donny didn't really think twice about it but to Rose, it was a big deal. Secretly she worried about what she looked like, what she should wear, what she would say. She decided she'd better play it cool or she might blow the whole thing.

The next night came and Rose went over to Donny's house. As he led her inside she spotted Donny's mom and asked, "Hi Mrs. Morris. How have you been?"

"Just fine, dear, and you?" Came the reply.

"Good. Thanks. Donny's gonna share some of his history smarts with me. We have a test tomorrow and it's not my best subject."

Susan Morris replied, "You're in the right hands. Donny's great at math but history's his second best. I'm sure he'll help you. See you later." She walked through the dining room toward the kitchen.

Donny said, "Okay, why don't we go upstairs to my room. That way no one will bother us."

"Fine," Rose said. But she was thinking about what other things could happen in his bedroom.

When they got upstairs Rose realized she'd never been in Donny's bedroom before. She tried to imagine what kind of things would be in it. Well, she was wrong. She pictured posters of music groups, sports stuff, maybe a lot of black and dark colors. Not exactly, that wasn't Donny. His room had light blue walls with slightly darker carpeting. His walls had a few posters of sports icons but there were mostly abstract prints by quality artists. She was pleasantly surprised. There was a guitar in a corner, a very comfortable-looking chair, a big bed with a red and blue bedspread with a maze-like design, and a desk with his computer on it. On the other side of the room there was a small television, some small speakers, and stereo equipment. Rose said, "Hey, nice room. I pictured some kind of Gothic cave-like womb, all dark and black and stuff. It's not. It's nice. You sure you live here?" She laughed.

"Yes, I live here. I like my room," he replied. "Well take off your jacket and let's get down to business huh?"

Rose removed her windbreaker. She didn't think Donny would notice the clingy top she chose for the night. "Probably a mistake," she thought to herself.

"You want to sit on the big chair, the desk-chair, or on the bed ... sit wherever you'll be most comfortable."

"I like the bed if you don't mind. I'll probably want to stretch out if it gets too boring."

"Okay," Donny said, "Go for it. I'll start out in the chair but, I'm warning you, if I start to get tired I may come join you on the bed to get comfortable." Rose felt a little chill run up her spine. She hadn't been this close to Donny with no one else there. She liked it.

They opened their books and began studying. This mainly consisted of Donny telling Rose what he felt was important about each chapter and what he felt she should know for the test. Rose was listening because she didn't want to appear stupid, but she couldn't help looking at Donny a lot. At one point he noticed her staring and he said, "Rose ... is it just my imagination or are you staring at me?"

"It's probably just your imagination. Besides, what else am I going to look at? You're doing all the talking aren't you?"

"Well yeah. I don't know. Forget it." Donny went back to reading from the book and asking Rose questions. Rose went back to looking at him but, now, she looked away every time he looked up.

Eventually, Donny started to yawn a little. He asked Rose, "Would you mind if I came over there with you? I'm getting a little tired in this chair."

"No problem," she answered. But her heart started beating a little bit faster.

Donny joined her on the bed and lay on his back with a pillow to prop up his head. She was sitting, cross-legged, beside him ... looking at him.

Donny put his book down on his chest for a minute and seemed to be off in his own world. Rose said, "What's up? Your mind appears to have left the premises?"

He said, "I guess so. Sometimes I just wonder where I'll be in ten years. I mean we're looking back at all this history and it makes me wonder where I'll be looking back from ten years from now."

"Where do you think you'll be? Where do you want to be?" She asked.

"I don't know," he said, thinking, "but I damn sure need to be with the right person. A lot of the other stuff doesn't seem to matter if you're not with the right person."

Rose's heart skipped another beat and she asked herself if she should let Donny know how she felt about him. The answer she kept getting was no, but it was tempting. She wanted so badly to ask him what he thought about her but she was afraid of being too forward. She decided to sneak up on the subject.

"So, Donny, what qualities would the right person have for you?"

He thought for a moment, and then said, "I'd like to think they'd be beautiful on the outside and the inside. You know, physically attractive, smart, clever, funny, generous, unselfish, blah, blah ..."

"Blah, blah? Hmm, pretty fussy aren't you?" Rose said. But what she really wanted to know was did Donny see even half those qualities in that airhead, Carla?

Donny said, "I don't know, Rose. Don't most people want everything in their soulmate?"

"Sure. But I think sometimes it's more about being a fit with the one you love. There are so many not-so-obvious parts of a personality that can attract or disgust you, right?"

Donny said, "I guess. Rose, what do you think is attractive about me?"

Rose took a deep breath and said, "Well, you're a sweet, sweet guy who's got looks, brains, humor, and most importantly I think you genuinely care about people. And I've just realized your second toe is longer than the rest. It means you're special ... destined for great things. Also, you're good on your feet in most situations I've seen. People would say you're pretty intuitive."

"Well thanks, Rose. I didn't know I was that intuitive. I don't feel that

I am sometimes. I don't know, most of the time I feel pretty average."

"You don't get it man. You're special. There are lots of girls who would kill to be with you." And then she couldn't help herself, "But all you seem to be able to think about is Carla. Why? What is it that's so incredible about her?"

Donny closed his eyes for a second and said, "Rose, that girl is a vision to me. I look at her from any angle, no matter what she's doing, no matter what she's wearing, and she's just beautiful." He had a stupid gleam in his eyes … Rose wanted to strangle him.

She frowned and said, "But what about inside? You said you wanted beauty outside AND inside. That chick wouldn't cross the street to help her own mother. She's a snob. She's nasty. And she's one of the most conceited girls in school. There, I've said it. Don't you see any of that?" Rose was relieved. At least she got her thoughts out of her mouth.

Donny said, "Look, Rose. I've never met anyone I've felt this way about. I don't know, maybe I'm overlooking some little quirks in her personality but I know that down deep she's got to be good. If she wasn't, God wouldn't have put her in such an incredible package." Rose was about to throw up but she controlled herself.

"Oh my God," Rose thought. "It's like he's infected with something. This guy who's normally really good at reading people is totally stoked by the outer shell of Carla. He's got a nasty, nasty crush that won't let him be objective. It seems hopeless."

When she spoke she said, "Well Donny I can't believe you are so taken with her looks. I just hope the fact that she doesn't seem to really know you exist eventually wakes you up." Then she decided to go for it and said, "So, what do you think of me? What are my good qualities?" She couldn't help it. She had to see what he'd say.

Donny said, "Well there's uh, uh … no, that's not it. There's, um … no, that's not really it either. I'd probably say that you were … well, no that's not right. Rose, I'm not sure you have any good qualities." He laughed … and she slapped him.

"You jerk," she said. "You won't even give me that?"

He sat up and faced her. Then he said, "Rose, you are one of the cutest, sweetest, funniest, brightest people I know."

Rose thought, "People, ugh, I'm not even a girl to him." And she thought she'd be fine if she never heard herself described as cute again.

Donny continued, "You are very special. That's why Joey and I spend so much time with you. We're almost best friends. And you know what else? You will find that very special person. A guy made just for you. But it'll probably happen when you're not thinking about it much. So just do what you do and wait. He's out there."

"He's ten inches away from me," Rose thought. "What do I have to do to make him see that he's the guy I need?"

Donny climbed off the bed and said, "I'm getting tired, Rose. Do you think you've got enough to do okay on the test?"

"I guess. I can go over it again when I get home. Thanks for your help."

Rose picked up her book and her notes and she quietly left. On the way home Rose pictured the evening ending a different way … with Donny taking her in his arms and pledging eternal love and devotion before he kissed her and made passionate love to her.

Donny's picture was slightly different. After Rose left he cleaned up, got into bed, and was instantly transported to a luxury master bedroom sometime in the future. Carla was there, in a silky negligee, coaxing him under the sheets. Donny went to sleep happy.

I had just entered the school cafeteria with Donny and we weren't sure we'd even be able to eat because they were scheduled to stop serving lunch in ten minutes. I was in a huge rush and Donny knew I'd have to gulp down my food and split. Fortunately, there was no line. We both got tuna melts and fries and grabbed a table near the windows. By the time I took my first bite we were the only people left in the large room. But then Carla came rushing in. Carla didn't really eat in the cafeteria much, and when she did it was usually with Rob. So it was unusual to see her by herself. She grabbed whatever was left in the display, put it on her tray, paid the cashier, and turned toward us. Donny felt his pulse quicken. Where else would she sit but with us, right? Right. She waved at me and came over to the table. I whispered to Donny, "Calm down boy. She's got no other place to sit and I've gotta' get out of here in two minutes."

Donny started to say something when I looked up and said to Carla, "Sit down, Banes. We're the only game in town."

She sat and said hello. "I got stuck talking to my dumb-ass Phys. Ed. teacher. He's such a moron. Plus, I think he's got eyes for me but don't tell Rob. He'd get very upset."

Donny just stared at her as she put a piece of tomato into her mouth.

I said, "Well I hate to eat and run but you guys are on your own. I'm already late for a meeting I can't miss so … see you later." I got up and walked away but I saw very uncomfortable looks coming from both Carla's and Donny's face. Neither was happy to be in that situation and they both had just started to eat so it looked like they'd be stuck there for a little while.

Donny was nervous. He took a bite of his sandwich and said, "So how're things with you, Carla. I don't see you around very often." He was just about ready to start sweating.

She looked up and said, "Y'know, I'm with Rob most of the time and we're usually out and about."

"Now what," Donny thought as he tried to keep himself from staring at those incredible eyes. After an uncomfortably long silence he said, "So you and Rob are exclusive, right?"

"Right," she said, "Why? Is there something I should know?"

Donny thought she might be fishing for some info about Rob and another girl … which wouldn't exactly have been beyond the realm of possibility.

"No reason really. Just making conversation. Just wondering if you ever date other guys." He was sorry about it as soon as the words left his lips. His solution was to put more food in his mouth.

Carla smirked a little. She looked at Donny and said, "If I didn't know better, Donny, I'd think you were going to ask me out."

Donny cringed. He said, "No, no. I was just curious … honestly. But, if you weren't exclusively with Rob … I, well, I might have asked. I'm sure a lot of other guys would ask you out. Would that surprise you?"

"No," she said, "but I AM exclusive with Rob. I don't have eyes for you or anyone else right now. Hope that doesn't hurt your feelings or anything. Besides, aren't you involved with that little curly-haired, elf girl?"

"Rose and I, and Joey for that matter, are just good friends. We hang out together." "God," he thought, "that sounded really dumb."

"How cute, a threesome."

Donny wasn't happy with the conversation and prayed for a change of subject but he was tongue-tied. He was saved when Carla said, "Well, it has been nice but I've got to go. Rob will be looking for me. Bye-bye."

"Yeah, bye," Donny replied and he watched her walk away. "She walks like a real woman," Donny thought to himself. Well, my friend Donny could be such a pathetic adolescent sometimes!

Chapter Three

It's not really that there was nothing to do in our town. It's just that once we got cars we could go other places … so we did.

One of my favorite places during the summer months was Lake Monroe Beach. I'll stop here and say that I know what you're probably thinking: big beachfront, beautiful white sand, and clear water. Well, not exactly.

Lake Monroe was a very large lake but it was just, well, a lake. It didn't have the beautiful sand that came with an ocean. In fact it really didn't have sand at all. It was basically just dirt. And there weren't huge areas of beachfront. They were just strips of dirt scattered along the lakeshore. Some were close to swimmable water. Some just bordered filthy lake water. But we had discovered our "spot." It was kind of out of the way but not too many people knew about the "spot." The water was reasonably clean. There were trees shielding the area so it wasn't obvious from the road. The beach itself had soft dirt and not much else. It was private, quiet, and kids could go there and not be bothered by anyone or anything. Also, there was a 7-11 two blocks away where you could get suntan lotion, drinks, and food.

Donny, Rose, and I started going there as soon as we could drive. It was only about ten minutes from town and it was a nice place to relax on a Saturday or Sunday afternoon. There were other people there but if we walked for a bit it was pretty private. We'd bring our towels, a radio, some food and drinks (we even snuck a few beers when we could, even though we were still under eighteen). We'd read, talk, listen to the radio, play Frisbee, sleep, swim a little, and sit in the sun. There was no place to change and no place to shower so we wore our suits under our shorts and had to wait for them to dry before we could leave. There were many nights we stayed late just to watch the sun set through the clouds over the lake.

The land the beach was on was technically owned by the town so once in a while a cop on patrol would drive by. But none of them ever stopped and asked questions or seemed the least bit concerned that we were there.

Donny, who was a Pisces, always told me that the water did something wonderful to him. He'd say there was something about sitting in the sun near the lake, listening to the water breaking across the rocks, and the sound of the wind, that gave him some kind of inner comfort. He was a happy guy when he was at the beach.

Rose, on the other hand, always had a struggle at the beach. She had this really white, freckled skin that didn't do well in the sun. She wore a lot of clothes and slathered sun block all over any body parts that were exposed to the sun. Poor Rose … she liked the idea of the beach. She liked the idea of the three of us going to the beach. She liked relaxing on the beach, having nothing she absolutely had to do. And she liked doing all of that near Donny. But she never quite got comfortable in the sun.

On some weekends, especially when it was cooler outside, we went into the city. There was a lot to do in Eastchester. We went there for all kinds of things from sporting events to restaurants. We couldn't afford the really fancy restaurants much but there were great Chinese and Italian restaurants like nothing we had in Lake Monroe. It just made us feel grown-up, I guess, to be able to make a reservation at a cool restaurant, spend an hour or so eating with all kinds of different people that we DIDN'T know, and then driving home.

We also saw some really good concerts in Eastchester. Bigger, more popular rock groups that would never come to Lake Monroe came through Eastchester. It was a big deal for us to get tickets to a rock concert and drive to the city to see it. Sometimes we'd eat at a cheap restaurant first and then go and see the concert. It was fun.

And then there were the sporting events. Lake Monroe high-school basketball and football were okay, but Eastchester had college basketball and football and some minor league pro-sports like baseball and hockey. Donny and I would go whenever we could afford tickets and had the time. Rose mostly passed on the baseball but she'd go to a lot of the hockey games. I think she liked hockey because of all the fights … and of course, it gave her more time with Donny.

Also, Eastchester had something they called an art movie house. It was a movie theater that showed films you couldn't see anywhere else. They were usually movies from other countries, or film festival winners. Sometimes they'd even show marathons by a single director or actor. The seats

were cheap and it was usually a lot of fun. Rose was the driving force here.
She loved anything different … especially foreign films. She'd see what was
playing in the papers and then she'd work on Donny and me until we'd agree
to go. The only thing I really hated were the films with subtitles. God it was
a pain to have to read a whole movie. But Rose and Donny didn't seem to
mind.

The beach and the city were fun trips but probably the coolest place
within driving distance was Kenworth State Park. Now that was really something special! I don't mean just because the Incident happened there. It was
just one incredible spot on the earth by any standards, and we were happy to
be living so close by.

It was about a half-hour's drive to Kenworth and every time we went
there it felt like a trip to another world. It just didn't look like anyplace else.

When you drove into the park you paid a fee at one of the gatehouses.
Then you drove for miles and all you would see would be trees, big sky, and
the winding two-lane road you were on. Eventually there were signs direct-
ing you to various parts of the park … Lower Falls, Middle Falls, Upper Falls,
campgrounds, cottages, restaurant, picnic areas, and some others. If you kept
driving you would begin to feel yourself heading upward. Slowly, but steadily,
the road climbed higher and swung to the right and the left and back again.
Eventually, if the leaves weren't yet fully populating the trees, you could see
beyond them to the gigantic gorge that split the earth at that spot. The gorge
was hundreds of feet deep, and if you looked closely, you could see that at one
end of it there were three sets of waterfalls. Each of these flowed progressively
downward and poured into a river at the lowest level. As you got closer you
could see the striated rock lining the gigantic crevice. It appeared that the
river's water had etched through the rock over many years and created this
masterpiece of nature by itself.

The park had many overlooks, which allowed visitors to pull off and
look over into the gorge at the falls and the river. There were many trails
which touched the overlooks that you could follow down the sides of the
gorge right into the waterfalls. Humans had carved steps up and down the
sides of the gorge, which allowed you to climb all the way up or down the
steep walls and even walk behind the waterfalls at each of the three levels.
There were many places to stop and sit on natural stone benches and huge

boulders, and a number of designated picnic areas with very primitive bathroom facilities were available.

The park was around 13,000 acres of land and you could drive to any one of the three waterfalls and make your way up or down, as appropriate, through the woods and along the great walls of the gorge.

Often when we went to Kenworth, Donny would enter his poetic mode and talk about how he felt so much a part of the world looking at all of this natural beauty. Rose also appeared blissful. The grandeur of the scenery made her feel romantic. She would have given anything to be there for a picnic, or in a rented cottage, alone with Donny. Personally, I can't remember any place I've been that's made me feel more healthy and stimulated than when I'd stand at the top of the upper falls at Kenworth, take a deep breath of the clean air, and look out over the tremendous power that nature displayed. It was incredible!

When we went to Kenworth it was generally an all day affair. Sometimes we brought picnic food and drinks. Sometimes we brought bathing suits and swam a little in the quiet parts of the river. Sometimes we were fully dressed with heavy boots for a long hike. We often took two cars just in case we wanted to split up and explore different parts of the park … or in case someone got tired early and wanted to go home.

Yes, Kenworth was special in many ways. But none of us could have ever imagined just how special Kenworth, and the Incident that occurred there, was about to be in our lives.

Chapter Four

On a warm Wednesday night in late May, Rose, Donny and I were in Donny's rec room shooting pool. Donny was a killer pool player, probably because he'd grown up with the table in his house. I always enjoyed playing Donny because I would always strive for that one game in six or seven where I'd win. Rose, well, she was just there to hang with Donny and me ... mostly Donny.

School was over for the year and we were reflecting on how we were going to spend the summer. Both Rose and Donny had told their parents they would look for part-time jobs, but neither had made any significant effort to actually find one. Although it was only for a few hours a week, I already had a job as a part-time clerk in the insurance office where my dad worked. But, right at that moment none of us was thinking about working. We decided that Sunday would be a good day to go to Kenworth Park. We usually went on Saturdays but on Sunday mornings the park would be relatively empty because many people were in church until about noon. If we got to the park early we would have it mostly to ourselves. That seemed to be a good idea until Donny remembered he promised his mom he'd go to church with them that Sunday. We almost postponed our trip but Donny said, "You know what? Why don't you two go up to Kenworth real early, stake out a cool place to hang, and I'll just meet you at 12:30 somewhere?" Rose looked at me and said, "I'm okay with that. Having the two cars means we can leave when we want without hassling anyone else." I said, "Fine," and it was a date.

I was up really early on Sunday. It was always kind of exciting to me to be heading for Kenworth, just because I knew how gorgeous it was there and how good I felt being there. I put on my jeans and a Grateful Dead T-shirt, my sneakers, and grabbed my baseball hat. I was ready for the day.

I went downstairs and ate breakfast alone. I liked it that way. One benefit was that I got to read the sections of the paper in the order that I wanted without having to worry about who had what section. When I was done I grabbed the keys to my mom's Toyota. Last night she'd said I could use it for the day. When I left to pick Rose up it was just 8:30 a.m.

Rose asked me not to ring the bell or honk the horn because she was afraid her folks might still be sleeping. They weren't big churchgoers. She was sitting on her front doorstep when I drove up. Rose had kind of a beach bag/backpack that she used whenever we went to the beach or the park. It was purple … and big. But the stuff in it was light so she had no problem strapping it on and going for hikes.

Rose also had a plastic bag with handles. It was from one of the clothing stores where her mom shopped. Rose had filled it with sandwiches, some cookies, pretzels and some drinks. I had two, six-packs of beer in a cooler in the trunk. Don't ask me why, I just did.

We were kind of quiet on the way to Kenworth. It took us no time to get there because the traffic on Sunday morning was practically nonexistent.

We paid our park fee at the gatehouse and drove for a few minutes. When we got to the first parking lot we pulled in and decided we needed to have a plan for where we'd go. We got out and immediately noticed the air smelled different in the park. I was never sure why (maybe it was the height or something) but it sure felt good to breathe there. We walked over to one of the picnic tables at the edge of the lot and I pulled out the big, foldable map we got when we paid our fee at the gatehouse.

Rose said, "You wanna' go all the way up to the Upper Falls today?"

"We've got time to do whatever we want. The only thing we've got to keep in mind is we told Donny we would meet him at Willow Overlook at 12:30. That's about half way between the Upper Falls and the Middle Falls," I pointed out.

Rose said, "That's such a beautiful spot. The trails run both up and down from Willow. It's a good starting point. We could meet Donny, head up the trail through the woods and find a picnic clearing with a great view while we have lunch."

"Sounds like a plan to me. We can take our time heading up there because we've got a few hours without Donny. How 'bout we drive up to the Middle Falls and hike a little. We can take one of those cool stone walking bridges across the gorge if you're not too afraid to do it," I teased.

"That's bull," she said. "It would take a lot more than a stone bridge to get me trembling in my boots … and you know it!"

I laughed. "I know it, just teasing a little. Once we get to the other side of the gorge we can work our way upward so we'll eventually wind up across from Willow Overlook. We'll just come back across one of the other stone bridges."

"Let's do it."

We drove the beautiful, leisurely route up the mountain taking in the gorgeous weather in upstate New York on a crisp May morning. Every so often we pulled off the road to take in a vista, shoot a photograph, or just stretch our legs. We stopped a few times, pulled off the road, and walked off the trail to get really close to the edge of the cliffs. It got higher and higher as we drove on, and the views became more and more dramatic.

We pulled into the parking lot near the Middle Falls and took our stuff out of the car. It wasn't a long hike and, honestly, I was looking forward to the exercise.

We started off on a trail that slowly wound upward toward our destination. We were taking our time because we could, and there was always a lot to see. It never seemed to matter that we'd been to that park many times. There were always new trails we hadn't known about, new vegetation and critters in the woods, undiscovered caves highlighted by spectacular natural lighting, and weather-etched alcoves in the sides of the cliffs. Often you might even see a real variety of people who could've been from anywhere.

One of the paths off the trail led right to the edge of the gorge and, about 50 yards up the side of the cliff was a fantastic old stone bridge that crossed the chasm at a narrow point. This walking bridge was only about 12 feet wide, and when you walked across it the views were mind-boggling. If you looked one way you would see the Upper Falls spitting foam and hydro-electric intensity from above, down in your direction. If you looked the opposite way, in the distance, you'd see the water rushing at incredible speeds toward the drop-off that was the Lower Falls. If you looked across the bridge you would see the beautiful cliffs with steps carved into the walls of the gorge, going both up and down on the other side. And if you looked down … well, you really shouldn't look down. The sight of the water rushing toward the Lower Falls at incredible speeds, hundreds of feet below you, was both exciting and frightening at the same time.

Many people would get to the edge of the bridge with every intention of crossing but, at the last minute, before they took their first step out, they made the mistake of looking down. I'd guess at least half of those people never took another step onto the bridge.

Rose and I didn't have that problem. When we got to the bridge we just kept walking side-by-side, right across the bridge to the other side. Then we turned around, looked back over the bridge and laughed. I suppose the laughter just relieved the tension.

We hiked for a while on the far side of the gorge then we sat down to rest and have drinks on some huge boulders that were conveniently located so they could serve as seats or tables.

"There's another stone bridge not too far up there that will get us back over to the other side, right?" Rose asked.

"Yes," I said, "It's just up that way," I pointed. "You doing okay?"

Rose said, "I'm fine. This couldn't be a more beautiful day, could it?"

"Nope … this was a good idea. Hey, there goes another one," I said, pointing to a man who was on a trail about 50 feet above us.

"There goes another what? It's just a guy." Rose said.

"Yeah, but look at how he's dressed," I said.

Rose looked a little more closely. The man was pretty far away but she could just make out his clothes.

"He's wearing a robe or something. And that's either a very weird hat, a turban, or some kind of dead animal on his head," she said, laughing.

"He had a big walking stick … did you see it?"

"No," she said. "But, it wouldn't surprise me. He looked like some kind of religious kook maybe."

I said, "Well it is Sunday morning and I know a lot of different church groups hold services outside at Kenworth on Sundays. They don't make you get a permit or anything … just as long as you don't bother anyone else."

We relaxed and talked for awhile and then, picked up our stuff and started hiking again. When we got to the second bridge we walked right across with no second thoughts.

"We're not far from Willow Overlook and it's 11:45," I said. "Why don't we just head up there and relax. Donny should be here soon."

Donny had gotten up a little late that morning and he had to rush to keep up with his family. His older sister Valerie had come home from college a few weeks before and she was going to church with them. Donny's mother and father were happy that the family was all there. This was the first time they'd all gone to church together in a long time. Donny had to take a separate car, and throw his clothes and some other things in the trunk, so he could leave and head straight for Kenworth when the service was over. He wasn't very good about cleaning out his car so when he opened the trunk he saw he'd left his old baseball bat, his glove, and even a basketball back there. He was too rushed to clean it out then so he just left it all, climbed in and drove to church.

He sat through the church service but he really wasn't paying any attention. His mind wandered from Carla to school to Kenworth Park and back again. Somehow, he managed to look like he was engaged in the service but he couldn't wait to get out and drive down to the park.

When the service ended he was one of the first people out the door. He got in his car and he was off. He cranked up the radio and was set for the 30-minute drive. On the way he fantasized that he was really meeting Carla and they'd spread out a blanket in a quiet clearing, eat and drink until they were full, and then hold each other - touching and kissing - until the sun was ready to set.

As he pulled up to the gatehouse of the park, the attendant waved and opened his sliding glass window.

"Beautiful day," Donny proclaimed.

"Yes, sir, where are you headed?" Asked the attendant.

Donny was surprised. Attendants don't usually ask where in the park people are going. They just take your money, give you a map and wish you a good day.

"I'm going up to Willow Overlook and then I'm not sure. Maybe Upper Falls, maybe Middle Falls. Why, is something going on?"

"Well, we don't want to alarm anyone but we just received a report about several wild dogs who were seen around the Upper Falls. They scared a family who was attending some kind of religious meeting. We've sent a ranger to investigate but I'd just urge you to keep your eyes open and be careful. You can't be too careful."

"Okay," Donny said as he handed over his money and took the map in return. "Thanks."

Donny drove off without too much concern. This was a very big park and there were all kinds of critters in the woods. It just didn't occur to Donny that there would be any trouble. But then, he wasn't aware that this was the day of the Incident.

Chapter Five

Before Rose and I even got to Willow Overlook we could see the magnificent view of the gorge it afforded. As we walked out near the edge of the gorge it felt as if we were as close to heaven as you could get. We sat down on a huge rock and just looked out over the waterfalls for a few minutes while we waited for Donny to show up.

I saw his old Buick out of the corner of my eye. He pulled into the parking area of the Overlook and got out. Then he went to his trunk, removed some clothes and pointed to the bathroom sign. He was going to change out of his church clothes.

When he came back, Donny was dressed in jeans, sneakers, and a football jersey. He said hello and walked over to us with a smile on his face.

"It is s-o-o-o good to be out of church and here with you guys," he said gratefully.

Rose said, "Yeah. Where do you guys want to go from here?"

I suggested we walk down to the nearby picnic tables, find one in the shade with a good view of the gorge, and have lunch. Everyone agreed.

We spent the next hour eating, drinking and listening to music on the radio. Donny and I threw the Frisbee for a while. Then Rose said, "Let's hike."

We took off in the direction of the Upper Falls. We walked out trails and up steps carved in the cliffs and rested for awhile on stone benches along the way. When we got near the Upper Falls we decided to walk behind them and we did. The paths allowed us to walk underneath the falls and look up and out through the incredible power of the raging waters pouring over the edge. We must have sat watching the water for 45 minutes before any of us wanted to move. The mist from the falls was getting our clothes a bit wet but we really didn't care. When we got up we headed up the cliff again, to the source of the falls above.

It was truly a magnificent sight standing slightly above, and to the side, of the Upper Falls and looking down to the Middle and Lower Falls … and the river all the way below. Again, we stayed for a long time, each of us realizing how lucky we were to have access to such natural beauty so close to home.

After awhile we headed back down the cliff, found a stone bridge and crossed over to the far side of the gorge. We hiked through woods and streams and came out back on a trail leading downward. Then we crossed another bridge back to the side of the gorge where we started. We had seen only two or three other people in our hikes that day. We were pretty far off the designated trails most of the time. It felt like a pretty cool adventure.

Late afternoon came and Rose began to tire a little. She asked if we could sit again so we did. I asked if she wanted to head back to the Middle Falls so we could get the car and go home. She thought that was a good idea because we had a pretty long hike back. Donny said he'd walk back to the Overlook with us and we could continue on down to the Middle Falls. It took us a little while to get there and when we did, Donny said he was going to sit for a while before he left. He parked himself on a big boulder overlooking the gorge and Rose and I said goodbye and began our trek back down to the car. Donny watched us disappear on the trail into the woods.

As the sun started to move low in the sky, the meeting ended and the small group slowly disbursed. There were bows and hugs and a language spoken that hadn't been heard in this country except by a rare few. The day at the park had been wondrous for them. They had come together from far away places to hear Kwajeh's words and listen to his teachings. But it was an unusual sight to people passing by the clearing near the Upper Falls that day. Men, women and children, mostly dressed in flowing robes, some with head-dresses or turbans, gathered around one man - Kwajeh - to listen and learn.

As the people walked off down the paths to the parking lots, Mehrak and Kwajeh were left alone. Both men wore long robes and sandals and had dark, wrinkled skin. Kwajeh was a very old man with snow-white hair and a beard, hunched over, and walking with the aid of a carved walking stick.

Mehrak was middle-aged and was acting as an aid to the older man. They spoke in whispers. In fact, sometimes it looked as if they were speaking with no sound at all coming from their mouths. Arm-in-arm, they slowly began to make their way down the trail by the gorge to the parking lot where Mehrak had parked their car.

As he sat on the large boulder Donny reflected on the earlier part of the day. He never really enjoyed church much but there was something comforting about being there together with his family ... especially when his sister Valerie was home. The two of them were not really very close but that was not because they didn't love each other. I think older sister - younger brother doesn't always work quite as well as older brother - younger sister. I don't know why that is but at least for Donny and Valerie, he somehow resented that she was the first-born, and Valerie would've been happier with an older brother to protect her and give her advice. As they grew up, those little inadequacies their relationship suffered from seemed less and less important. Then, just as they were growing closer, she went a few hundred miles away to college and Donny only saw her when she was home for vacation. The last few times she was home Donny noticed that they seemed to have more to say to each other and Valerie became more and more open about her friends and her life at school than she had been. The result was Donny opened up to her about his life more and I'm pretty sure that, if they had the opportunity to spend more time with each other, they would become much closer.

As Donny looked out over the great gorge his thoughts wandered to Carla. Somewhere, on a much deeper level, he recognized that some portion of his feelings for her were mostly physical. I mean, he really didn't even know her that well. He just felt that tingle when he saw her and it was tough to resist. Donny made himself believe that, if they ever had the chance to be together for a period of time, Carla would finally succumb to his charms and be his. He asked himself if he was kidding himself. His answer was always, "No. It's possible. I just need a chance with her."

Then, as he was daydreaming, Rose came into his mind. He really hadn't spent much time thinking about Rose. I guess he kind of took Rose for granted. He was blind to her feelings toward him and I didn't think telling him how she felt would do either of them any good. The truth is, though, Donny and Rose would have been great together. They were a cute couple physically. Their personalities very much complimented each other. And neither of them realized that they thought alike on most important issues. She was just so into him that sometimes she had trouble relaxing and being herself. And Donny was so caught up in thoughts of Carla that there wasn't any room to let Rose in. I thought it was sad but I didn't see what I could do about it.

Donny felt very comfortable sitting on the boulder at the overlook and didn't really want to move, but with the sun going down and the air cooling he knew he'd have to leave soon. He closed his eyes and took a deep breath. That's when he heard the scream...

Kwajeh could not move very quickly because of his physical age. Mehrak was very patient, taking his arm and guiding him down the trail, through the woods toward the parking lot. They were approaching a turn in the trail that was totally open to the gorge and the falls because there were very few trees there. Mehrak wanted his learned friend to experience the beauty of the gorge at its best so, holding tightly to his arm, Mehrak guided Kwajeh to the edge of the cliff where the full vista of the gorge and its falls was unobstructed. He stopped for a minute to allow Kwajeh to take it all in before they moved on.

It was then, out of the corner of his eye, Mehrak thought he heard something moving in the brush near the trail. As he slowly turned his head his nerves froze in his body. He was looking at something so frightening it almost stopped his heart.

It probably used to be a large bulldog or a mastiff ... a very powerful breed of dog. But that's not what it had become, not what it was that day. An immense head was attached to a powerful body with dark black hair that was matted and blood-soaked in splotches. There were gashes and what were probably oozing bite marks all over its body and paws. Its giant face was swollen and distorted; looking like it was in spasms of pain. One of its eyes was bloodied and almost shut, the other ... bright red. Its foaming mouth hung open revealing large, knife sharp teeth, and a steady drooling stream of bile mixed with blood was dripping from its face. From somewhere down deep in its throat there was a steady, sorrowful, low moan and wheeze. And then it growled. It was the angry, chilling, guttural growl of a horribly rabid dog stalking its prey. And it was moving, slowly, closer toward Mehrak and Kwajeh from 20 feet away.

Losing all control from the sheer terror of the moment, Mehrak held tightly onto Kwajeh and involuntarily screamed at the top of his lungs. He screamed the word, "Help" over and over. He and Kwajeh were trapped with no place to go. Behind them was the gorge with a certain death drop into the falls and rocks below. Facing them was a massive, drooling rabid monster which had them fixed in his sights.

Donny's head whipped around the moment it registered in his mind that someone was calling for help. It took him an extra second because even that simple one syllable word had to be deciphered through the accent of the man screaming it.

He knew it wasn't coming from very far away so he jumped off the boulder and started onto the trail at a pretty fast clip to check it out. When he heard the second scream he stopped in his tracks, decided he'd better bring something to protect himself just in case, and ran back to his car. He opened the trunk, looked around, and grabbed his baseball bat. He ran back to the trail and moved on into the woods.

As he ran, the cries for help intensified. He could hear the terror in the voice but just couldn't imagine what could be causing it. As he got closer he found himself behind what appeared to be some kind of large animal. Beyond it were two older men, clad in robes, backed up to the edge of the gorge. This animal had them cornered and was stalking them.

Donny thought for a second and realized that, unless this thing somehow got scared and ran, there was no stopping it without wounding or killing it. He also recognized that if he did nothing, both of the men would be torn to shreds or pushed over the cliff to their deaths. And he wasn't blind to the danger he himself faced should this beast turn on him. It was terrifying but he knew, right at that moment, all three of their lives were in his hands. He tried to stay calm and shouted, "Don't move," at the two men, then very slowly walked toward the animal. The beast stopped in its tracks and turned it's head when it heard Donny's sound behind him. Donny recognized clearly that this would make the dog turn on him but it was all he could do … he was the one with the weapon. He walked slowly toward the dog with the bat raised above his head, both hands gripping it tightly. When the dog turned around it roared at him and more blood and drool spilled from its cavernous mouth. It dug its rear legs into the ground and leapt forward from 30 feet away. It would take seconds for it to reach Donny so he crouched sideways and steadied himself into a baseball batter's stance. It would give him full power to put his entire body behind a swing at the beast's head. At that moment he also prayed. The dog was racing toward him with his mouth open, a huge row of sharp teeth exposed. When it was about four feet away it leapt into the air directly at Donny's face. Beyond being frozen in terror, Donny stood his ground, pulled the bat back with both hands, stepped forward with his left foot and swung the bat around using the full force of his body to slam it into the huge head of the rabid dog in midair. Fortunately, his timing was perfect. The momentum of the swing rotated Donny's body all the way around. But he had felt the enormous impact of the bat crashing against the monstrous skull of the dog as it crushed the bone and brain tissue inside the animal's head. He would never forget the sharp cracking sound and the screech of the rabid animal as its brains were splattered all over the ground. The animal's momentum had caused its hideous body to fall on Donny and, even without most of its skull, tremors kept it moving. Donny struggled out from under it and smashed it twice more with the bat to be sure there was no further threat. The animal stopped moving. Donny could breathe again.

At first, the two men had been huddled together watching Donny, immobile and in shock from the terror. But the older man, Kwajeh, had gripped his chest moments before Donny's perfect swing ended the animal's life. Kwajeh fell into the arms of his friend Mehrak. He was having pains in his chest and had trouble breathing.

Donny took one look back at the dead animal, and approached the two men.

"Are you okay?" He asked them.

"I am okay, my friend, but Kwajeh, my teacher, is ill. I believe it may be his heart. We are in the middle of nowhere. What can we do?" Mehrak asked.

Donny thought quickly. He knew there was a park exit just past the Upper Falls and then a quick, 10-minute ride to the ER at Boynton Hospital. Donny said, "Help me carry him to my car. We can get him to a hospital that is close by. It will be okay. Come."

The two of them half supported, half carried, Kwajeh to Donny's car and loaded him into the back seat. Donny got him a bottle of water and all three of them took off for the hospital. Very little was said on the trip to

Boynton but Donny learned a few somewhat mysterious things about the men he had just saved. Kwajeh was some kind of religious leader from a middle-eastern country. The word "Shaman" kept coming up from Mehrak but Donny wasn't real sure what it meant … just that it was somehow mystical. Mehrak was an old friend and a disciple of Kwajeh's. They had come from an annual conclave of followers from around the world. Although there were only about 30 people there, apparently they represented some of the most important international followers of Kwajeh's teachings. It was chance that their conclave was in Kenworth that day. It happened because a key disciple had rented a cottage in Kenworth every summer for years and recommended it for the meeting. Donny didn't really know, nor did he want to, much about what it was that Kwajeh taught. He thought it was just fine that they all got out of the situation alive.

When they got to the hospital Donny drove right around to the ER. He ran in, yelled for help, and watched as they admitted Kwajeh. He told Mehrak he'd stay long enough to see how Kwajeh fared but that he'd have to go home soon after. Mehrak insisted that he stay until Kwajeh could express his thanks personally however long that took. That made Donny a little nervous - what if the guy didn't regain consciousness until tomorrow? But he figured as long as they were all in it this far he may as well be around to see if the guy was okay. He went down to his car, retrieved the clothes he'd worn to Church sans the sport jacket, and went to a washroom to cleanup and change. When he came out Mehrak was sitting in a waiting room in front of a window, praying.

Chapter Six

Donny and Mehrak sat in the waiting room for less than a half an hour when a Doctor in scrubs appeared. He said, "Are you the people who brought in the gentleman in the robes?"

"Yes, it was us," Mehrak replied.

"I'm Doctor Moore and we're going to need some information about the patient, but I can tell you that he will be fine. In fact, well, he's quite remarkable. He had all the symptoms of a heart attack, which could have proved very dangerous in a man of that age. But, before we could actually treat him he appeared to be recovering spontaneously. I would recommend he remain here overnight for observation and a few more tests."

Mehrak said, "Yes, he is a very remarkable man. His ability to overcome illness is truly amazing. I don't think he will want us to keep him overnight but I'd like to spend a few minutes with him now. May we go and speak to him?"

"Yes," said Dr. Moore, "but keep it short. He really should rest and we really feel it's in his best interests to be tested further. We should be sure that he is out of any danger before we release him."

Mehrak nodded and he motioned for Donny to follow him. They walked down the hall to the room Kwajeh was in. He was alone and had an IV and some wires from monitors attached to his body.

Kwajeh's eyes were closed when they entered. Donny was somewhat uncomfortable with these men and didn't quite know what he should say … so he thought he would just listen. But, as he stood there with Mehrak at Kwajeh's bedside he heard very little. The two of them appeared to be communicating in a language that Donny didn't recognize. They never spoke to each other in normal tones. They were more like whispers. It was all very strange and Donny thought it would be good if he could just get the heck out of there and go home. He really wanted to take a shower and lie down.

Mehrak turned to Donny and said, "Please, Kwajeh would like you to come closer to him. He will speak to you and I will translate so you will understand."

Donny said, "Okay," and, swapping places with Mehrak, he stepped to within inches of Kwajeh. He looked into the now opened eyes of the old man and thought, for a moment, that he saw movement - movement, like planets circling around the sun. It was dizzying. He had to close and open his own eyes again to get his bearings. It was very strange. Kwajeh removed his unencumbered hand from underneath the covers and reached out for Donny.

"Please take his hand," Mehrak said, "It is alright."

Hesitantly, Donny lifted his own hand and took the old man's hand in his. It was small, gnarled, and hairy, but very warm. Donny just held it … but it gave him chills.

Kwajeh whispered to Mehrak in their strange language, and Mehrak spoke his translated words:

"Kwajeh says … you are an exceptional young man. What you did today, for two strangers you did not know, was beyond kind. It shows you have a heart that is pure and a mind that works as swiftly as lightning from the sky. You put your own life in peril to save ours without the slightest hint of hesitation. For this we will be eternally grateful."

The old man squeezed Donny's hand tighter. Mehrak continued:

"Where I come from, the gift of life is indeed the most holy and sanctified of all. He who gives it shall be praised and revered above all others. You are owed a great measure of gratitude for preserving this precious gift for two men whom you do not even know." The old man paused and closed his eyes. After a few seconds Donny thought maybe it was over and they could go, but Kwajeh's eyes re-opened and, again, he whispered the strange words to Mehrak.

This time though, Mehrak's expression changed. He began to look somewhat surprised as he listened. After a few more words, the surprised look on Mehrak's face turned into one of concern. He took a breath, turned to Donny and said:

"Kwajeh is a very holy man, a man of powers beyond the understanding of most human beings. He is far older than he even looks and the powers and abilities he has within him have evolved from a distant beginning over a very long period of time … centuries in fact. It is beyond my humble ability to explain them or even fully describe them. All I can do is communicate his thoughts and ideas to others. It is not for me to judge their implications. With that in mind please, know that Kwajeh has chosen to reward your remarkable behavior with one of the most extraordinary gifts within his power."

Donny couldn't believe what he was hearing. Who were these guys? Why was this happening to him? "Maybe I should just say goodbye and leave," he thought. But the old holy man in the bed and his translator mesmerized Donny. He just stared at Kwajeh and listened as Mehrak went on:

"For your goodness Kwajeh has chosen to grant you the power to know other people's thoughts." Mehrak stopped for a second to let Donny absorb the words. Donny wasn't sure what they meant.

He tried to gently let go of Kwajeh's hand, which he'd been holding all this time, but the old man's grip was insistent.

Donny said, "Um, excuse me, what did you say? The power to know other people's thoughts? Yeah, that's what you said, right? Look, I'm really happy I was there at the right time to help you two out but, well, the power to know other people's thoughts, um, seems a little too generous a gift, you know? So, maybe I should just head on home and leave the two of you to rest and recover from this horrible day." Donny was thinking that perhaps the two of them were really wackos and he was taking this whole thing a bit too seriously. Again he tried to gently weasel out of the old holy man's grip. But again the firmness was unrelenting.

Mehrak continued, "I understand, my friend. It would, of course, be difficult to believe that such a thing exists if you were not aware of Kwajeh's power. I know that in a short period of time you will prove the truth of Kwajeh's gift to yourself. All I can do is convey Kwajeh's words and explain that there are caveats (you might call them strings) attached to the gift."

"What do you mean?" Donny asked. He had no idea what any of this meant.

"First, the gift may take a day or two to materialize. You will know it when it does. Also, Kwajeh would like to urge you to put it to good use. Change lives for the better. Help people. Do good things. He wants you to understand that although you may use the gift as you choose, these are the intended uses of the gift. And lastly, the gift may not be permanent. You will have a period of several months to enjoy your blessing. At the end of that period of time you will be given a choice of keeping the gift or giving it up. Because of the immense power the gift affords you, if you do decide to keep it, it will be at some sacrifice to you. Kwajeh will determine the degree of sacrifice required to keep the gift. This will all be explained by him at the appropriate time."

Donny's jaw felt as if it was hanging open as he tried to absorb all of this. He didn't really know what to make of it yet. The most plausible explanation was, again, these two were nuts and he should just forget them. But reviewing the last few things Mehrak said, Donny replied, "How would Kwajeh contact me. Aren't you two going back to whatever country you came from? You don't even know my last name or where I live!"

Mehrak smiled, "Kwajeh will contact you. Do not worry. Instead, focus on how best to use this new power with which you will be blessed. It is not as simple as it sounds. But remember, it is a blessing Kwajeh has bestowed on you because you have shown that you are an exceptional young man. Use it well."

At that moment, Donny felt the old man's grip relax. As he looked into Kwajeh's eyes he thought he saw motion again. This time it was the huge foaming waves of an ocean crashing into the shore. It was so vivid Donny was awestruck. He stared for a second, and then dropped his hand to his side.

Mehrak had turned toward the old man and Donny thought this was the time to leave. He said a quiet, "Thank you," turned, and left the room bewildered. He heard no objections.

On the drive back to Lake Monroe he went through the events of the last few hours and it felt like a dream ... as if it had happened to someone else. But he looked down at his body and saw the bruises and felt the sore muscles where the rabid dog had landed on him. Everything was still in his mind, clear as a photograph, but he still wasn't sure if it was real ... and if it was, what did it all mean? This was the Incident. It would change Donny forever.

Chapter Seven

When Donny walked into his parent's house his mom was in the kitchen.

"Donny, is that you?" She asked.

"Yes, ma, it's me."

"We pretty much gave up on you for dinner. It's so late. I thought you were going to Kenworth with your friends … what happened? Everything okay?"

"Yeah, everything's fine. I just got hung up talking to some people. Sorry I'm so late."

"No problem. But Joey called. He seemed to think you would've been home a few hours ago. I was concerned."

"Again, sorry mom. I'm filthy … I'm gonna go upstairs and take a shower."

"Okay, sweetie." She hadn't even looked up at him.

Donny went up to his room, quickly changed out of his clothes and went in the bathroom to shower. He let the hot water linger long over his sore body. It felt good as it relaxed his muscles from the strain of the day. In his mind he kept reviewing the Incident as if he'd find a new take on it, but it kept playing out the same way. He just didn't know what to make of it. He didn't feel any different. He wasn't hearing anyone's thoughts. He promised himself he would try to just forget the whole thing happened.

After he got dressed he went downstairs to get something to eat, as it had been a long time since lunch. While he was sitting in the kitchen the phone rang. I was on the other end.

I said, "Hey Donald, what the heck happened to you? When I called before your mom said you weren't home yet. I couldn't imagine where you went. "

"Well, it's kind of a long, strange story."

"Everything okay?" I said.

"Yes. I think so," came Donny's answer.

"You sound a little strange, man. What's going on?" I pressed.

"It's a little too weird for the phone. Let's wait till tomorrow and I'll tell you the whole story. Just, for now, don't say anything to anyone else … even Rose. Okay."

I said, "Yeah, okay. I wouldn't know what to say. You sure you don't even want to give me a headline?"

Donny said, "Fine. I saved a Shaman's life and he gave me the power to read minds. Got it?"

"A what? Oh," I laughed. "Why didn't you say so? I knew it was something simple like that. No problem. We'll talk tomorrow," I laughed again and hung up the phone. A Shaman? Right!

Donny put the phone down and finished his food. He went back upstairs and turned on the TV but he wasn't really paying attention. He was still trying to figure out just what it was that really happened to him that day.

Donny slept well that night. He woke up late to the sounds of his sister Valerie's stereo. He rubbed his eyes and sat up in bed. What day was it? What was that strange dream he had last night? As he went into the bathroom he began to remember the events of the day before. Was it real or was it a dream? He felt his stiff muscles tighten as he stepped into the shower. Yep. It was real. At least he thought it was real.

After his shower Donny dressed and went downstairs for breakfast. But before he could eat he just had to satisfy his curiosity. He walked through the kitchen, said "Good morning," to his mother and walked right out to his car parked in the driveway. He put the key in the trunk, took a breath, and opened it. There, right where he'd left them yesterday were his stained clothes from the park and, his baseball bat, tinged with blood he knew came from a rabid dog. It was real! Jesus.

After breakfast the phone rang and it was me again. I wanted some elaboration of Donny's day yesterday and I told him I was coming over. He said, "Fine," and hung up.

About an hour later I arrived at the Morris house and rang the bell. Valerie answered and invited me in. Since I hadn't seen her since the last time she was home from college, we talked for a while. She told me she was dating a new guy. Someone named Tony Donato. I wondered silently if Tony was any relation to the Donato family who'd been in the news a while back regarding certain racketeering rumors. Anyway, she seemed to really like this guy, Tony, and who was I to ask such a personal question, right?

Donny came downstairs and we all sat together for a few minutes. Then Donny asked if I wanted to play some pool in the rec room. I said, "Sure," and I said goodbye to Valerie and walked through the hallway to the rec room.

Before Donny kicked my butt in pool I thought I'd ask him about yesterday. I was still puzzled by his long absence and I really wanted to know where he was.

Donny said, "Joey, I really want to tell you what happened but, well, I just don't think you're gonna believe me."

"Don't be stupid, man. Why wouldn't I believe you? What could be so bizarre that you would even think that? C'mon. What happened?" I was getting tired of asking.

"Okay, here it is," Donny said. And he proceeded to spew the elaborate story of the Incident at the park, Kwajeh and Mehrak, the hospital, the gift and the rest.

When he was done I found myself just looking at him. "Oh for Christ sake, Donny, why would you even make up some ridiculous crap like that? C'mon!" I was still looking at him, waiting for him to break into a smile and then laughter. It didn't happen. He just kept looking down. I walked over to him and said, "Donny. What's going on? Why the story?"

Donny said "Come with me," and walked out into the hall. I followed him as he walked outside and popped the trunk of his car open. He pointed and I looked inside. Holy shit! The clothes he was wearing yesterday were lying there covered in what look like blood and some other filth. And then I saw his baseball bat. It, too, had blood on it. I just stared for a moment, and then I looked up at Donny. Was it true! Sure seemed like the part about the rabid dog was.

I said, "Donny, that's amazing. Are you okay? Are you hurt at all?"

"No I'm okay, just a little sore and scratched up from that beast landing on me."

But it was the rest of the story, the part about the holy man and his friend that had me curious now. I thought about my time with Rose yesterday and remembered, "Donny, while Rose and I were hiking toward the Outlook yesterday we saw a guy with a turban and robes in the trail above us. He sounds like he could've been one of the people from your Incident. That's incredible."

"Incredible," Donny mimicked.

I said, "What about the gift, the mind reading part? What the hell was that? Did that really happen? Do you feel anything from it? Can you hear my thoughts?"

Donny said, "Don't know. Yes. No and No."

"Huh?" I said.

"I don't know what it was. Yes it really happened. No I don't feel anything at all from it. And I can't read your thoughts. Hold that. Are you thinking we should drive over to Angelo's for lunch?" Donny said.

"Sorry man. It didn't even cross my mind. But that is some really strange stuff. You know, I read a little once about a Shaman. They were mystical holy men in the Middle East somewhere. I think Persia before it was Iran. I think they could talk to the dead and, maybe, they were, like, healers.

In any event they were scary. Was your guy scary?"

"I wouldn't say scary, just really, really old and, like, mystical. I don't know, man, I never felt anything like I did when I looked into his eyes. I saw planets and oceans … it's … it's hard to explain. Anyway, I don't feel any different today so I'm pretty sure it's a load of crap."

"Okay buddy but that's just weird. You going to call the park rangers and tell them about it?"

"Actually," Donny said, "the fewer people that know about it, the happier I'll be. I don't want to have to answer a lot of questions and be interviewed on TV and stuff. Also, I don't want kids talking about it like I'm some kind of hero at school. So do me a favor … I'm going to throw the clothes and the bat away at the dump and I'd prefer if you wouldn't mention anything about the Incident to anyone. That includes Rose … okay?"

"I guess so … if that's what you want."

"Great," Donny said, let's head over to Angelo's. I need to start thinking about something else."

The rest of Donny's day was uneventful. He and I ran into Carla and Rob leaving Angelo's. I could see the pain of one-sided love come over Donny the minute he saw her. It was just sad how he had no control over his feelings for her.

Donny had dinner that night with his parents and Val at a Chinese restaurant. The food was great but for some reason the wait staff just reminded Donny of the Incident. It seemed like it was going to take him a really long time to forget about it.

He got home and decided to call Rose. I think he was really just fishing around with her to make sure I didn't tell her anything. We had agreed that since she didn't know he got home late from the park that day it wouldn't be necessary to create any kind of story for her. Donny talked to Rose for a while and, inwardly, she was thrilled. She loved it any time Donny called her, for any reason.

Lying in bed that night Donny wondered how long Kwajeh and Mehrak stayed at the hospital. Where did they go? How did they get their car from the park? Blah, blah … sweet dreams.

When he awoke the next morning he went to the bathroom to take a shower only to find the door locked. He knocked and heard Val on the other side: *I need my own damn bathroom. Sharing one with my little brother sucks.* Donny said, "Well you don't have your own bathroom. I guess you'll just have to share with your little brother."

Val opened the door with a puzzled look on her face and said, "What are you talking about?"

"What you just said?" He replied.

"Um, no, I didn't say anything. But that's what I happened to be thinking. Weird!"

Donny was a little surprised. "You didn't just say you wanted your own damn bathroom and sharing with me sucks?" He asked. She looked at him like he was crazy, "No-o-o. I gotta' go. I'm hungry."

A little unnerved, Donny went in to take a shower. But something didn't feel quite right. He couldn't put his finger on it. Maybe he just wasn't fully awake yet he thought.

After his shower he dressed and went downstairs to have breakfast. Val and his parents were already at the table eating. As Donny pulled out his chair and sat down his dad said, "Don, can you do me a favor and pick up some caulk at the hardware store this morning. I've got a busy morning and we need to fix the tiles in the guest bath a little later."

"No problem," Donny said.

Then his mom said: *It's about time Ed did something about those stupid tiles. It was incredibly embarrassing the last time we had friends over. Sometimes he's just so lazy it gets me angry.*

Donny was looking at his mother when he heard her say that, and the thing was... her lips didn't move!!

"What the hell was that?" Donny thought to himself. "I heard those words from my mom just as clear as could be … but she didn't actually say anything. Jesus!" Donny turned white. Then he looked at his Dad and heard: *If I have Don get the damn caulk maybe that'll shut Susan up for a while. She moans about everything.*

But Ed Morris didn't say anything out loud either. "Unbelievable," Donny thought. "What the hell … ?" Then the Shaman's words from two days ago came back to him as clearly as if he was sitting in the hospital room right then, "Kwajeh has chosen to grant you the power to know other people's thoughts."

"My God," Donny thought, "is there any possibility, any remote chance, that this is … is the gift? It can't be, can it?"

But Donny had heard Valerie's thoughts upstairs, and he had heard both his mother and father's thoughts without them saying a word. As hard as he tried he couldn't fathom another explanation … he was reading minds.

Donny was so shaken he had to excuse himself from the table and go upstairs. When he said, "I don't feel that well. I think I'm gonna lie down for a few minutes his mom said, "Oh Don, what's the matter? Are you okay?" She thought: *What now? Do I ever get a chance to rest?* Donny captured it all but he just couldn't believe it. He marched upstairs and threw himself on his bed. He needed to think. That was no problem … the thoughts were racing in his head. "Is this real?" he thought. "How the hell is it happening? Will I be like this forever? Can I hear everybody's thoughts? Are some people immune? Do they have to be in the same room as me? Will my head get so full with everyone's thoughts in a huge crowd that it'll explode? Shit! This is amazing."

As he lay there on his bed he realized that he was no longer hearing his family's thoughts … maybe because they weren't right there. That was a good clue. Perhaps because he wasn't focusing or aiming his mind at them. He didn't know. But he was damn sure he was going to find out how it worked. This was unbelievable.

He decided to experiment a little. He wanted to see if he could read someone's thoughts over the phone, so he called me.

"Hello," I said.

"Hi," Donny responded. "What's up?" He said, hoping to receive a head full of my thoughts.

"Not much," I said. And then there was silence.

Donny said, "Let's get together later ... maybe go to a movie."

"Okay ... you check the show times and I'll just come over in about an hour."

"See ya," Donny replied, disappointed that he had no inkling of what I was thinking.

"So", Donny thought, "it looks like I probably can't beam in on anyone over the phone. Or maybe Joey's just immune to my gift." "Gift," he thought, "is that what this is?"

He got up off the bed and went downstairs. Val was sitting in the living room looking at a magazine. Donny thought he'd start there and see if her thoughts just came to him or whether he had to somehow focus on her. *This is going to be a boring day if all I've got to do is read this crap.* It just came to him -- from Val. He heard more of her thoughts and then he thought he'd see if he could control it. He tried to turn her off ... and it worked! "Terrific", he thought. "I can tune people out." To be sure, he focused back on her and got: *What's he standing there for?*

"Donny, what're you doing?" She said. "Bingo," he thought, "I can turn it on and off. This could be really cool when I get used to controlling it."

"Just thinking," he said. He had an idea ... just for fun.

"Hey, I'm working on a trick. Pick a number from one to ten." He instructed.

"Five," Val said.

"No, no. Don't tell me what it is. He got: All right, 1. She said, "Got it."

Donny thought, "This is too easy." "Is it three?" He offered, purposely not wanting to arouse her curiosity.

"No," she said.

"Well what was it?" He asked feigning ignorance.

"It was one but how could you possibly know. Needs a little work, don't you think?"

"Yep, sure does." Donny smirked.

"What are you doing today?" He said, and waited for an answer, focusing on her.

He got: *I wish I could be with Tony, in bed, all day. That'd be great.*

"Shopping," she said.

"This is gonna be great," he thought to himself.

A few moments later the phone rang. He walked over and picked up the receiver. He tried to sense who it was … nothing. It was Rose.

He said hi to Rose and tried to pull in her thoughts. Nothing came. She wasn't in front of him. "That must be one of the rules," he thought.

He told Rose that he and I were going to the movies and invited her along. She agreed to meet us at his house a little later.

They had decided to go see some foreign film that Rose was all excited about. To do that we would have to take the short ride to Eastchester's art movie house.

I got to Donny's house before Rose. When Donny let me in we went right into the rec room and decided to play a rack or two of eight ball.

Donny had decided to tune out my thoughts until he wanted to hear them. He and I were playing pool just like we usually do. Then Donny "aimed" his mind at mine and, apparently, he could hear all of my thoughts.

Donny was very quiet so I asked him if anything was wrong. He said, "No, just trying to wake up. I was up late last night." But what Donny was really doing was learning how to filter another person's thoughts. After a little while Donny could turn me on or off with no effort. He broke into a smile. Again I asked him what was up. Again he said it was nothing.

When Rose arrived we had to leave for the drive to Eastchester. Donny opened his mind up to Rose and he was more than a little surprised with what he got.

Donny was driving and Rose was sitting next to him in the front. I was behind Rose in the backseat.

I was talking about some of the colleges I was considering and sort of rambling on.

Donny's brain was focused on Rose. He got: *Donny is so cute today. God I'd like to hold him close and wrap him around me. Ugh. I need to stop feeling this way. He'll never come around as long as he's under that witch's spell. But maybe someday, something will open his eyes. I'd be so much better for him than her. She probably won't ever let go of Rob anyway. What a waste.*

"Holy crap!" Donny thought. "I had no idea she felt that way. None. What do I do about it? This is a dangerous gift to have. Could be very dangerous." It was only right then that Donny began to truly realize that he would be hearing many things that weren't meant to be heard. Some things would be tremendously interesting or helpful. Some would reveal incredible lies. He would have to be very, very careful how he used this, how he acted and reacted, whom he told, what he told them. "God," he thought, "what have I gotten into?"

The next time Donny looked over at Rose he saw her in a slightly different light. He thought she was a wonderful friend and a terrific person. He felt sorry, and a little bit guilty, that Rose felt as smitten by him as he himself was with Carla. A little light went off when Carla came into his mind. It was accompanied by a sinking feeling. He would have to listen to Carla's thoughts about how inconsequential he was in her life and probably how crazy she was about Rob.

The more Donny thought about his new power, and how heavy a burden it actually placed him under, the more he knew he had to share it with someone. His parents and sister came into his mind, but after very little thought he realized the one person he really needed to share his gift with … was me.

Chapter Eight

After the movie we drove back to Lake Monroe and dropped Rose off. I went back to Donny's house for a couple of games of pool. Donny was unusually pensive. I could tell he had something on his mind. As Donny grabbed for the rack to start a new game, I said, "You've been acting a bit funny today … especially toward Rose. It's like you're being extra nice to her or something. What's going on?"

Donny put the balls in the rack, lifted it straight up, walked around the table, and fired off a break shot. The balls flew in all directions. Two of them went into pockets. Donny didn't say anything other than, "I'm stripes."

"Okay, I said. What is it? Is it still that stuff from the other day? C'mon."

Donny put the bottom of his pool cue on the floor and stood up straight. He had a tough time getting it out but he said, "Joey, remember what I told you the old men said in the hospital?"

"Yeah, pretty much, you mean about them being grateful and giving you a gift? Sure. What, are you reading minds all of a sudden?" I said, jokingly.

The look on Donny's face as he looked into mine held the amazing answer. "I can hear other people's thoughts," he said slowly.

I looked at him, knew he thought he was serious, but, well really! How could that be? I said, "Everybody's thoughts? Some people's thoughts? Whenever you want to? C'mon, Donny, you don't really think..."

"Shut up Joey. I'll show you. Let's start with something simple. Pick a number from one to … never mind … ANY number. Just think of one number, as many digits as you want. Think of it."

I thought for a few seconds and had the number 3437 in my head.

This was ridiculous. No one was capable of ...

"3437," Donny said.

I almost wet myself. "Jesus," I said, "that's it. How ... how did you know that? You are scaring me."

"Well, I just sort of turn my focus up to allow your thoughts to reach me and I can hear what you're thinking. For example, right now you're thinking that, still this is some kind of trick, but less and less ... right?"

"Right," I said. It was hard for this to sink in. My best friend Donny could read minds. He could hear what people around him were thinking. Incredible!

"Can you hear everyone's thoughts? Does it work on a phone? What about someone on TV? Can you send your thoughts back to them? God, this is unbelievable."

"Here's what I know so far ... I've only tried it with a few people. I can tune people in an out if I'm with them. I've been able to shut it all off easily when I want. It doesn't seem to work on the phone. And, I don't think I can send my thoughts to them ... it's one-way."

I just stared at him for a second. I thought for a minute about what it would be like scoring 35 points in a basketball game then, before I could ask Donny what he thought I was thinking he said, "So you want to score 35 points in basketball huh?"

"Shit!" I said, "I'm not sure I'm gonna like you knowing everything I think. Maybe this isn't such a good thing, but it sure as hell is incredible!"

"Well ... I don't listen to every thought. I can't think that fast and have my own thoughts too. Also, I would imagine in a room with a bunch of people, I'd have to be very selective about whom I listen to or there'd be too much input. I can't believe this is happening. Joey ... this IS real, right?"

"Oh yeah, buddy, it's real. I just wonder how you're going to be able to use this, and what you're going to use it for? I guess one obvious thing is you'll pretty much know when someone is lying to you -- telling you one thing and thinking the opposite."

"Uh-huh. But this is going to require some serious discipline on my part. There will be people that don't like me, that maybe want to harm me, or someone else for that matter … if they're thinking it in front of me, I'll know. I'll have to figure out how I will handle that. It's pretty delicate stuff, y'know?"

"Right. Talk about a life changer," I agreed.

Then Donny said, "And of course there's the ethics and maybe the legality of being able to do this. I mean, I will know what people are thinking before they say it. That could be huge. I'm just starting to realize how big this is."

"Big!" I said. I didn't know what else to say.

Chapter Nine

The next day we went to lunch with Rose at Angelo's. I knew Donny hadn't been with a group of people since he became telepathic and he was anxious to see what it felt like. While we were driving over to pick up Rose, Donny wondered if we'd see Carla and if she'd have thoughts about him that he could hear. He was a little bit nervous because he knew he didn't mean anything to Carla and I think he felt he was about to get hurt by her indifference or maybe even her negative thoughts. When we picked Rose up I wondered if Donny was listening in to what she was thinking. And, I wondered if she was thinking about him. Poor Rose. She had no idea her feelings for him were now an open book. I silently hoped she would be thinking of other things that day so she wouldn't be that revealing to Donny.

When we got to Angelo's we took a booth in the middle of the restaurant. Donny was looking around, checking out who was there. Mitch Corwin waved from a few tables away. He was sitting with some guys I didn't know. The waitress came over a few minutes later. It was Joann, one of the regular waitresses. She said hi, dropped off the menus and left. I looked over at Donny and he was quiet. Rose started talking to me about one of her friends and some college guy this girl was dating.

Donny listened to see what kinds of thoughts he was picking up. There were bits and pieces from different people's minds. He had to sort of open and close his receptors to let in only certain thoughts from certain people, otherwise his mind could get flooded with too much information at once.

Joann, the waitress, came back and said, "Hi guys, what can I get for you?" Donny got: *How come there are always three of them? Which one does the girl belong to?* Rose ordered a tuna salad sandwich on white with French fries and coleslaw. Donny ordered a cheeseburger with fries. And I ordered chicken salad with melted cheese and tomato on white. Donny heard Joann think: *chicken salad with cheese and tomato on rye.* Joann picked up the menus and left quickly. Donny said, "I think you're gonna get rye bread instead of white."

Rose asked, "Why do you think that?"

Donny caught himself, "Um, well isn't that how most people order it? I dunno."

I looked at Donny and pretty much knew he heard her thinking the wrong order. I really couldn't wait to see what Joann brought me. This was amazing.

As we were waiting for our food, Mitch Corwin and his friends were leaving. He stopped by the table to say hi to Donny … he knew him from math class. Donny said, "How're you doing, Mitch?"

Mitch said, "I'm good. What's up?"

"Nothing much," I said, "just having some lunch."

"Are you guys going to Sue Fagin's party tomorrow?" Mitch asked. Donny got: *Bet they're not invited.*

Donny, who was invited, said, "Don't know yet. Are a lot of people going?"

"Carla told me almost everyone who is home for the summer's going. Sue's parents are away for a week … should be a blast." Mitch said.

I said, "Well, maybe we'll see you there." But Donny knew I was thinking: maybe we won't.

Mitch waved goodbye and left. Joann arrived with a tray of food and Rose got her tuna sandwich. Joann gave Donny his burger and fries. Of course when she put my chicken-salad sandwich down in front of me, it was on rye bread. I was ready for it and touched her arm, "Uh, Joann, I ordered this on white." I said as nicely as possible.

Joann whipped out her pad, thumbed through the orders and said, "I wrote down rye. You sure you didn't say rye?" She asked. Donny got: *Why is he yanking my chain. He ordered rye.*

"Yes, I'm sure. Ask Rose … Rose, what did I say?" I asked for confirmation.

Rose said, "He ordered white, Joann." Donny nodded his head too.

Joann said she was sorry, scooped up the plate and said, "It'll be another minute."

Rose looked at Donny and said, "How did you know she'd do that?"

Donny said, "I told you. Simple mistake. Lots of people order it on rye."

I chuckled. Rose and Donny started to eat their food and, out of the corner of my eye, I noticed Rob Talbot walking in the door. Carla was right behind him.

When Donny first saw Rob and Carla he got a little bit nervous. This was one of the moments he was waiting for. Would Carla have some thoughts about him? What would she be thinking about Rob? Donny was just anxious to know a little bit more about how her mind worked.

Carla and Rob sat down several tables away from us. They didn't even see us at first. Rose said, "Well, there she is, guys. Donny, you going to melt or something?" Donny purposely tuned out Rose's thoughts just then. He didn't want to know. "No," he said, "but we should stop by their table and say hello."

"I guess," Rose said reluctantly.

When we finished our food we split the bill and the tip then got up from the table. We could see that Rob and Carla weren't talking much. I wondered if they could be having an argument since neither had happy expressions.

The three of us approached their table and I said, "Hi guys, what's for lunch today?" Donny immediately focused on Carla and got: *Oh it's them. Please don't stay long.*

Rob said, "Just having some burgers. What are you guys up to?" Donny looked at Rob and got: *Well, I don't really give a shit but I'll ask.*

Donny said, "Same as you. Just had lunch. May go up to the beach this afternoon. How're you doing, Carla?" He said directly to her. She said, "Fine." Donny was surprised that he didn't get anything from her, other than what she'd just said. He had noticed that people aren't always thinking and sometimes there's just nothing there, but he expected Carla to have some thought about them. But then it came. Carla thought: *Rose is such a little bimbo. I wonder if she's sleeping with both of them, or maybe just Donny Morris. He's kind of a little dummy too but he might be kind of cute when he grows up. They're pretty boring.* Donny thought, "It could've been worse."

We all said goodbye and the three of us left. When we got outside Rose asked, "How come I seem to be the only one that thinks that girl is the world's biggest phony? Don't you guys see through her act?"

I said, "I'm not sure I know what you're talking about, Rose. She's a bit of a snob but, other than that, I don't see the big problem."

And Donny chimed in, "She's beautiful, and smart, and all that stuff. What's to see through?" But he sort of knew what Rose was talking about. He felt that if he had more time to listen to Carla think he'd find out that she was kind of a well, a challenge.

Rose was typically disgusted, "I get it. You're so wrapped up in her looks you don't care about what's beneath. Well, believe me, you guys will figure it out someday. I just hope you don't get hurt in the process."

As we were getting into the car I said to Donny, "How'd you get invited to Sue Fagin's party anyway?"

"Oh, she's in my biology class and we've been talking a little. I bumped into her about a week ago and she told me about it. I just forgot to mention it. She did say I could bring friends. She wants it to be really big … you know, the party of the summer. You guys want to come?" Donny really didn't have to ask but, of course, he did.

Rose immediately said, "I don't think so. Too many people I don't care about or like will probably be there."

I said, "I'll go. I think it'll be fun. How 'bout we go together?" Donny nodded okay.

Looking forward to another chance to exercise his newfound telepathic abilities, Donny was excited about the party. He knew he'd want to be fairly close to Carla for a while to check out her thoughts, but he also thought it'd be fun just to watch all those people interact and hear their thoughts intersect.

I dropped by and picked Donny up that night and he was in a good mood. I said, "What will this night be like for you with all those minds for the picking, all around you? You lucky dog."

"We'll see," Donny said, "I'll let you know if there are any fantastic revelations but, if my experience so far is any indication, don't count on any great revelations. Most of the things I've heard people thinking about so far are pretty ordinary and not surprising at all."

I asked, "Have you been listening to Rose's thoughts lately?"

"A little," came the guarded answer.

"And have you learned anything you didn't already know?" I said.

"Yes. But you already knew. Why didn't you ever tell me that Rose had a thing for me?"

I sighed and said, "You know, you are both my friends and I thought it would be better if it just took whatever course it was destined to. I know Rose would probably be embarrassed if she found out you knew the extent of her feelings, but Donny, Rose has had those feelings … well, forever. She has always felt that way about you."

Donny took that in, then searched my mind for some other hidden truth, and didn't find anything. He never really considered Rose in that way. He certainly loved specific things about her but, being so into Carla's looks just didn't allow him to go any further. For a moment, he pondered the thought of a different kind of relationship with Rose but it was just a moment.

He looked at me and said, "Look, I know I'm only seventeen but every time I see Carla I don't really care about anyone else. And now, I've got this power in my mind. I don't know, it makes me think I might be able to maybe have things I never could before. It might mean anything I want is possible."

As I heard him say those words I immediately got frightened for my friend. I knew I could never really understand what it felt like to be telepathic, but I also knew that being able to read people's minds could be a very dangerous thing. It was right then that it first occurred to me that if he didn't use that power wisely he could create a mess for himself and others. This wasn't the time but I knew I would have to help him focus his gift on some of the right things. How easy it would be to get into trouble.

We could hear the music from Sue Fagin's party before we even got out of the car. There were cars parked all along her street and it sounded like people were outside in her backyard. We walked up to the house and rang the doorbell. In a minute, the door opened and Sue, smiling, welcomed us in. Donny heard her think: *Oh good. Donny brought that guy Joey with him. He's cute. I'll definitely talk to him later.* She led us into a very large family room with three sets of French doors leading out to a deck and large, treed backyard. There must have been 70 or 80 people there, and it was still pretty early. I saw a bunch of people I knew from school and a lot of people I didn't know at all. They were sort of hanging out in little groups who knew each other or wanted to meet each other. Some had sodas or beers in their hands and a few looked like they had mixed drinks. And in the backyard there were a couple of people who, from the smell, appeared to be smoking marijuana.

Donny looked around and decided to let his mind receive anything the people in his immediate area were thinking. He wasn't really sure how he'd match thoughts with the people thinking them but he would see what happened.

He heard different things from different faces in the crowd:

What the hell am I doing here? Why did I let Judy talk me into this? These people are...

Who is that chick? Look at those boobs? God, I'd like to....

I love you so much! I'm so glad we are together. Please don't look at other women ... I'm all you need.

She must be on a diet or taking some serious medication. She never looked that thin before.

I've got to find a way to speak to him. He'll notice me if I talk to his friend.

There's that jerk David. Look at that stupid chain he's wearing. Does he think he impresses us?

"Whoa," Donny thought to himself. This was kind of fun but a little too intense. Donny didn't want to hear everything from everybody so he decided to just focus on one or two people at a time.

I left Donny in the family room to get a beer in the kitchen. Sue tapped me on the shoulder and said, "I don't know if we ever really were introduced. You know I'm Sue ... and this is my house. And I know you're Joey Evers, Donny Morris' friend. Welcome."

"Thanks, Sue. This is a beautiful house. Looks like it'll be a rockin' party. I was just heading to the kitchen to see if there's any beer."

"In the fridge, of course." Sue was looking at me with big blue eyes in a cute round face. I liked her right away because she seemed like she wanted to be with me as soon as we met.

I grabbed a beer out of the refrigerator and asked if she'd give me a tour. She said, "Sure. Just let me check on things in the backyard for a minute. Wanna' come with me?"

"Let's go," I said as I followed her back into the family room. I noticed that Rob and Carla had apparently come in from the backyard and were sitting on one of the family room loveseats. They didn't look particularly happy. Same faces as in Angelo's the previous day. I told Sue I'd meet her outside and walked over to Donny who was talking to a girl I didn't know.

I said, "I'm taking a house tour with Sue. By the way, Rob and Carla are sitting over there by the window." Donny turned and looked. I walked through the room and out the nearest set of doors. Donny decided he needed to get close enough to Rob and Carla so he could do his magic.

There was a group of people standing just behind the loveseat that Rob and Carla were seated upon. One of them was Mitch Corwin. "Perfect," Donny thought and he walked over to Mitch and said hello.

"How are you, Morris?" Mitch said. He introduced the two other guys he was talking to and went back to his conversation, but he made room for Donny to stand next to him and be included in the group. Donny was standing just three feet away from where Rob and Carla sat. He could hear them talking to some girl whom Carla knew. She was standing in front of them. Donny really wasn't interested in their conversation because he was focusing on Carla's thoughts and, to a lesser degree, Rob's.

There were large periods of time in the thoughts that he was hearing that Donny began calling "daydream time." Everyone seemed to have these. These apparently occurred when people were thinking unimportant, fleeting thoughts. They came in and out of their minds quickly and seemed to be forgotten as soon as they materialized. Carla and Rob were both having a lot of these … and Donny was learning to tune them out. He was developing a kind of automatic filter that sifted through the content and only honed in on the stuff he might be interested in. He was proud of himself for being able to do this.

After a few minutes of DD time (Donny's new name for unimportant day-dreaming thoughts), he heard Carla and Rob talking about one of the girls in the room. Rob was saying (out loud) how much better looking she was with a suntan. Carla disagreed saying that nothing the girl could do would hide her bad skin. "Besides," Carla added, "She's got a body like a brick."

Rob said, "You must be kidding. Her skin looks great and that girl is very sexy." Donny heard Rob thinking: *She's probably better in bed than you, Carla. I bet 75% of the girls here are.* Then as Carla shot Rob a dirty look, Donny heard her thoughts: *You are such an asshole sometimes. If you want other girls, just go do it. It's not like I couldn't have anyone I wanted. I don't even know why I'm spending all my time with you. I must be bored.*

Donny liked this. It was getting good. He was hoping Rob would do something else that was stupid so Carla would really get mad at him. Then maybe Donny could swoop in and rescue her. Right! Donny thought he should at least say hello to them so he turned around to the back of the loveseat, tapped Rob on the shoulder and said, "Hey Rob, How are you man? Hi Carla." They both looked up and said hello. Donny's receptors were in high gear, waiting for reactions to him. From Rob he got nothing. But then Carla thought: *Donny-boy. Here you are again … you seem to be around a lot lately. I wonder if this guy has eyes for me. Of course he does. Maybe I'll do a little flirting and get Rob a little jealous … Nah, maybe not.* Donny got excited for a brief moment. Then, with her thoughts, it went away. He asked if they'd been out back. They said they had and told him there were some people dancing on the deck and some people smoking dope under a tree. Donny decided to take a look for himself, but he definitely intended to come back. He wasn't done with being inside of Carla's head.

When he walked outside he spoke to a few people he knew from school. Everyone looked tanner and happier because it was summer vacation. They he walked down the steps at the back of the deck toward the people who were sitting and standing under the big weeping willow tree. The smell of marijuana was obvious. Someone asked him if he wanted some. He said no thanks but he looked around and didn't particularly like what he saw. There were two guys there who looked older than the rest. He'd never seen them before. They both had scruffy beards and weren't dressed like they were going to a party. They sort of stayed in their own corner passing a joint back and forth. They were whispering to each other but Donny could hear some of their thoughts.

First he heard one think: *Getting in here was a breeze. Just walking around back was a good idea. No one saw we didn't come in the front door. We should probably do this soon because the bigger the crowd the less people will notice us going inside and upstairs.*

The other one thought: *Who made Luke the boss? I'll do whatever the hell I want, whenever I want. I've got the knife don't I? If he gives me any trouble I'll just tell him to shove it.*

Donny froze for a second. "These two creeps had snuck in and were planning to rob the house … or worse. Shit! What should I do? I've gotta warn Sue."

He slowly turned around and walked back up the deck into the house. As he went through the living room he saw Sue and me coming down the stairs. Just as he got to us I said, "Hey man, what's the matter? You look like you've seen a ghost."

Donny said, "Sue this is really important. Can we go into another room and talk for a second where no one will hear us?"

Sue looked surprised but said, "Yes, I guess so. Come into the den … it's right over there." She pointed and both Donny and I walked toward the den. When we were inside Donny shut the door. He turned to Sue and said, "Sue, I don't want to freak you out but I've got to tell you what I just … uh, heard. There are two guys out in your backyard. Both are bad looking, older. One of them has a knife. I overheard them talking about sneaking in here and going upstairs when it's most crowded. I'm pretty sure they're planning on robbing your parent's house!"

Sue instantly displayed a look of terror. She lost her breath for a second. I looked at Donny and said, "Are you sure? You overheard them?"

Donny looked at me and I thought: *You read their minds didn't you? They didn't actually say anything, did they?* He heard my thoughts and just shook his head, yes. I didn't think I'd ever get used to that.

I said, "Sue, you've got to call the police. Even though those guys haven't done anything yet if the police show up they'll scare them. They'll probably run."

Then Donny said, "You know, you may not even have to call the police. I have another idea. Are any of your friends the people out back smoking pot?" He asked.

"I don't think so," Sue said, calming herself down. "My friends don't do drugs."

Donny continued, "What if you turned off the music, went outside and announced that the neighbors have called and told us they've just called the police, who should be here shortly. You can say the neighbors smelled the pot and got very upset. They're good friends with your parents and just wanted to warn us the police were coming. My guess would be those guys would split in a second the minute they heard the cops are coming. We could watch them. If they disappear the party could continue on. I doubt they'd come back. Or you could really call the police … whatever makes you more comfortable. Either way, you need to do it now, before they come inside."

Sue said, "I like your idea … I think I'll scare them. I don't really want the police to come if they don't have to, but I can't take the chance that something bad will happen here. Can you guys tell some of the other guys that you heard those two saying bad stuff and ask everyone to keep an eye on them?"

"Sure," I said. I grabbed Donny and we started to move around the room telling people we knew well about the two bad guys. Sue walked over to the stereo and turned off the music. She opened the glass doors, stepped onto the deck and said, "Everybody, please listen up. My neighbor just called me to tell me they've called the cops. They smelled marijuana and heard the loud music and they got really nervous. The police are on their way. If there are any of you smoking pot out back you need to leave … now! If you don't there's a chance the police will be talking to you soon, and I don't want any trouble at my parents' house. I'm sorry to mess this up for the rest of you but I think it'll be okay if you hang out until after the police go." She stepped back inside and stood next to the two of us. "Good job," I said. Donny nodded his head. He was watching the back of the yard where the two guys with the scruffy beards were. He saw them both talk for a second and then move very quickly toward the side of the house. Donny ran through the house to the front door just in time to see them emerge from the side yard, run out into the street and to a car parked on the other side. They got in and left in a hurry. Donny knew they wouldn't be back.

Problem with that solution was that about one-third of the guests also left. Donny found Sue and I and said, "Those guys are gone. They left quickly as soon as you mentioned the cops. I saw them get into their car and drive away."

Sue said, "Thanks so much for keeping your ears open and telling me, Donny. You may have saved us from a major catastrophe." Donny nodded, "No problem."

Sue and I walked around the room and told the remaining guests that the neighbors actually were just warning us that they would call the police if the pot-smoking continued. Since it was getting cool anyway, she suggested that everyone come inside the house and continue the party there. The remaining guests came in, Sue shut the doors and turned on the music. A lot of people were asking about the two guys.

Donny felt a tap on his shoulder and turned around to see Carla smiling at him. "What was that all about?" She asked.

"Well I overheard these two guys talking about robbing Sue's house so we had an idea to see if the cop story would scare them away. They left in a big hurry." Donny said proudly.

Carla said, "Really? That's pretty cool. Whose idea was it to make up the story?"

"Mine," Donny replied. He was blushing slightly.

"Nice," she said, "Good move." Donny searched her mind for other thoughts. There weren't any. She turned and walked away back toward Rob. Donny was trying to think of a reason to get her to stay and talk but he was too late.

Sue came over and said, "Donny, I really owe you for that. Thanks again." Donny shrugged. He started to think about what had just happened. He'd been given this gift just a couple of days ago and already he'd used it to do something good. He was proud of himself. "Maybe that's why Kwajeh gave it to me," he thought. "Maybe it's supposed to be used this way. I don't know, I guess I'm going to find out."

Since school had been out for summer vacation I didn't have the daily workouts I got with the basketball team and I started to feel as if I was letting myself get too out of shape. I tried working out at home but I didn't feel the motivation I needed to do it right. So, I thought about joining the gym for a few months till school was back in session. I went over to BodyFit, a health center where some of the kids from school belonged. They gave me the complete pitch and showed me around the facility. They had a pretty good discounted summer program for athletes from the high school who wanted to stay in shape for the summer. That was perfect. I signed up for four days a week and began the next morning.

I'd been there for two days and was on a stationary cycle on the third when Carla Banes sat down next to me on another bike.

"What're you doing here, Joey?" She said.

"What do you think, Carla? Waiting for a bus."

"Seriously, Evers, how long have you been coming here? I've never seen you before."

"Right, this is my third day. What about you?" I said, noticing how good she looked in her little exercise outfit.

"I've been a member here for almost a year," she said, "it's a great way to stay fit when there's nothing else to do."

"We'll see. They've got pretty good equipment here. I hope I can stay motivated enough to come four times a week," I said.

"You care about how you look, don't you?" Carla asked.

"Of course. And I know you care about how YOU look." I snorted.

"Right," she said. "Hey that was interesting the other night at Sue's party, huh?"

"Yeah," I said, "Looks like Donny did a really good thing for Sue."

"Uh-huh. That was pretty clever. He seems like such a shy guy. Is he a smart guy?" She asked.

"Hey. First of all, he's my best friend, so if he wasn't I probably wouldn't tell you anyway. But, in all honesty, he's fantastic. He's a little shy around you because, well, some of us get shy around women. But he's smart as hell, witty, clever, honest … all the good things. He's a hell of a guy, really!"

"So why do the two of you hang around with that little Rose girl? Can't you guys get your own women?" She said in her own, patented snotty-Carla way.

"Very funny, Banes. Fact is Rose is top drawer. I think she's very cute; she's funny and fun, and smart, and loyal too. The three of us hang around together because we like each other. Simple as that."

"Really, and neither of you are sleeping with her? Or is it both of you?

"You can be really obnoxious without trying, can't you? Like I said, we're all just friends. What's going on with you and Rob these days? Perfect life? " I asked.

"No … nothing special. We're together. But, to tell you the truth, I'm a little bored. Don't take that the wrong way but sometimes I wish life wasn't so perfect. Appearances can be deceiving." She was smiling but somehow she didn't look that happy.

"See you later, Joey. I'm going for a swim." She got off the bike and walked, like a movie star, into the woman's locker room.

Donny's mom, Susan, was really into antiques. They had a lot of antique furniture in their home and she was constantly shopping for little pieces of this and that. But her favorite time was the first Saturday of every other month. That's when a private auction company brought several rooms full of good to high quality antiques to the ballroom of the Radisson hotel in Lake Monroe. People came from many smaller towns and some even from the city of Eastchester to bid on this stuff and Susan Morris wouldn't miss it for the world. But since her husband would never go, she'd usually drag Donny with her. He didn't like it but she insisted … so he went.

The auctions were really well attended events, mostly by upper middle class women like Susan. Donny usually felt out of place but because his mom felt Donny had excellent intuition she involved him in the bidding process. Donny actually had amassed a fair amount of knowledge about antiques and he felt like he was making a contribution when he made suggestions to his mom.

But that day he didn't quite realize the contribution he was capable of making. That is, until he started reading people's minds at the auction. He just sat, listened, and watched for the first few items. He was hearing the thoughts of the bidders before and during their bids. So, when Mrs. Kramer bid $125 for the antique chest, Donny heard her think: *That's it for me. If they want it they can outbid me. Not a nickel more.* And when Mrs. Lewin and Mrs. Dolan were in a little bidding war over an antique silver service Donny heard Mrs. Dolan think: *I could go double her bid on this. I won't let it go.*

Donny was having a great time. He was telling his mom what these people were thinking, but saying that those were just his guesses based upon his intuition. His mom was impressed and proud of him. In fact, the woman sitting behind the two of them was equally impressed. She heard him say, "Mrs. Kramer's gonna stop at $125," and "Mrs. Dolan can probably go double that bid. I can feel how much she wants the silver." The woman thought to herself: *What a smart and intuitive young man he is,* and, of course, Donny heard her think it. He smiled to himself.

After awhile, Donny began helping his mom make bids with his own suggestions. And his mom was getting the things she wanted. "Donny was always helpful," she thought, "but today, well, he's a genius."

The item his mom wanted most was an antique secretary with beautiful curved glass. The bidding was to start at $500. His mom was excited. As soon as the bidding began Donny looked around the room at the people who were interested. He heard one thinking: *I have to have this. I've got up to $1,100 left to go for it.* As the bidding progressed from $500 to $550 to $600 to $700 then to $800 and $900, Donny said to his mom, "How badly do you want this, mom?"

She replied, "It's really the main reason I came today. It would be perfect in the den next to the club chair."

"How much are you willing to part with?" He asked.

She said, "$1,000. That's it. It's my top." She answered.

He thought for a moment and said, "Mom, I'm pretty sure that won't get it done. I've got a strong feeling that the lady up front will go higher than that."

His mom said, "Don, I know you've got a great feel for this stuff and you've been a genius today, but I've been doing this a long time and I'm confident that $1,000 will do it."

"$925," Susan Morris yelled out. The auctioneer asked for more bids.

Donny said, "You're wrong, mom. You will be outbid and disappointed I think." He was sure. He had read the other bidder's mind.

She wrinkled her brow at him as the competing bid came, "$950."

It was just the two of them now. No one else was bidding. The auctioneer said, "$950 to the lady in blue. Can we get $975?"

Susan Morris looked at Donny and said, "$960." She was confident she was almost there.

The auctioneer said, "$960. We've got $960. Will the lady up front go $975? $960 going once ..."

"1,000," came the bid from the front. Susan Morris' jaw dropped. She couldn't believe the other woman went right to $1,000. "Darn," she said to Donny, "you think I can just edge her out with $1,025 because I can't go any higher?" She asked him.

"$1,000 going once," came the voice of the auctioneer.

"No," Donny said, "You'll have to go over $1,100."

"$1,000 going twice," the auctioneer said menacingly, and he raised his gavel.

Susan Morris couldn't believe she was wrong and didn't want to spend any more money.

"Sold," said the auctioneer, "for $1,000 to the lady in the front row."

"Sorry mom, but I told you," Donny said.

Donny felt a tap on his shoulder. It was the woman sitting in the row behind them. She whispered, "Son, I couldn't help overhearing the ideas you were giving your mother during the auction. You have remarkable knowledge and intuition about antiques for someone your age. Can I ask how did you learn so much about these things?"

Donny half-smiled and said, "I come to these auctions with my mother whenever they're in town and people tell me I just have great insight. It's fun."

"You certainly do. I know your mother's proud of you. By the way, what's your name? I have a daughter about your age."

"Donny Morris," came his reply, "and this is my mother Susan."

"Hello," Susan Morris said, "Yes, Donny was quite amazing today."

"Nice to have met both of you. I'm Elaine Banes. My daughter's name is Carla."

I hit the gym at 7:30 a.m. on a Wednesday morning and it was already half full. It looked to me like BodyFit had a pretty good thing going. I changed my clothes, did some stretching and then worked out with the free weights for a while. I was ready to elevate my heart rate so I went over to the treadmills. And there was Carla.

"Hi Joey, getting that mean machine in shape again today?" She said hopping onto the treadmill next to mine.

"Hello Carla. Yes, wouldn't want to lose my manly shape would I?"

"Right. So what've you been up to lately?"

"A little bit of this, a little bit of that - beach, movies, pool, workout - you know."

"Yeah, I know. Summer in Lake Monroe, could it be more boring?" She complained.

"I suppose that depends on how you look at it," I replied.

Carla said, "So how's your friend Donny Morris doing?"

I was surprise she asked I said, "Oh he's terrific. He's the man."

She said, "I'm beginning to see what you mean. You know my mom was at an auction last Saturday. She sat behind Donny and his mother. She couldn't believe how much he seemed to know about antiques ... but more than that, how good he was at the whole bidding thing at the auction. My mother asked me if I knew him ... said it was almost like he was reading people's minds."

I choked a little on that comment. Was it becoming obvious already that Donny had a gift?

I said, "Yeah, Donny has been going to those auctions for a long time. He really knows how they work and how people bid. Like I've said, he's a very intuitive guy."

She said, "Well, maybe I'm missing the beauty of Donny. I guess I just didn't get it."

I said, "Hey, what's with you and Rob. Trouble a-brewin' or some-thing?"

She shrugged her shoulders, "I don't know. Just hasn't been the same lately. Maybe I'm bored, or maybe I'm just looking for something different. Lake Monroe can do that to you, you know?

"Yes, I know," I said. But not when your best friend is telepathic.

"Val, Tony's here," Susan Morris yelled as she ushered Valerie's boy-friend in the front door. Valerie's mother hadn't met Tony Donato yet and she was anxious to see the guy her daughter had been dating at college. Tony was a nice-looking guy with jet-black straight hair, a long face with bushy eyebrows and a little mustache. He was older than Susan would have liked … maybe 22 or 23, but definitely not college age. He had a long sleeved white dress shirt on with khaki pants and black shoes. He was wearing some kind of small medallion hanging from a gold chain around his neck. It wasn't big or ostentatious; it just contributed to the slick image of Tony Susan got on first glance.

As Donny walked into the front room from the kitchen he looked out the window and saw the convertible sports car out front. "Cool car," Donny thought. "Wonder what Tony's all about. From Val's description he's unlike any of the guys she used to date. Val said she met him in a bar and he's in his dad's recycling business. She says he treats her like a queen. I guess we'll see."

Susan Morris asked Tony if he wanted anything to drink. He de-clined. They both noticed that he had a kind of rough, New York City accent. A little thug-like. But, even so, Donny was really trying not to prejudge him.

The doorbell rang again and Donny opened it to find Rose. They were going to the beach together. As Rose stepped inside, Donny's mom introduced her to Tony. He said, "How ya doin'? Rose, huh? Pretty name." Donny resisted the temptation to read his mind just yet. He wanted to see what Tony had to say.

Val came down the stairs looking freshly made up. Even though he wasn't exactly dressed for it Rose and Donny were going on some kind of picnic.

Susan said, "Why don't we all sit down for a few minutes in the living room. We can get to know each other a little bit." Everyone nodded and followed Mrs. Morris into the next room.

Once everyone was seated and she'd checked on any drink requests, Susan asked Tony, "So, Tony, Val tells us you're in your dad's recycling business. How do you like it?"

Tony wriggled a little uncomfortably in his seat and answered, "It's fine. The demand for recycled goods is just starting to grow and my dad's also got a waste disposal business. The two of them sort of fit together."

Donny said, "Did you go to college at State, like Val?"

"No, actually I didn't go to college. I went right to work for my dad. I have two older brothers who also work with us in the business. It was sort of preordained since we were little kids. We were gonna grow up and work in our father's business."

Donny felt a little bad for Tony, who was now officially being subjected to a round of "20 questions" … until he opened up to Tony's thoughts. The first flurry of random thoughts he got was: *That Rose chick is cute. Mom's nice. Val - get me out of here. These people will never mind their own business. Why is her brother asking about my school? Am I not good enough for his sister or something? How much more of this bullshit do I need to put up with? Better not be this way every time or Val can kiss my ass goodbye.*

Donny shut it off. He got the picture. This guy felt like he was being attacked. He looked over at Rose and got: *Val's boyfriend looks like he's a wiseguy. Donny, let's get out of here.*

"Why don't we leave poor Tony alone? We've done nothing but batter him with questions since he walked in." Susan said.

Tony looked relieved and said, "That's okay. Val and I have to go anyway. We're meeting some of my friends at one of the parks a few towns over." He stood up, motioned toward Val to come with him and said, "Nice meeting you guys. See you later." Val picked up her bag, waved, and the two of them were out the door. A few seconds later the car started up and the sound of burning rubber screeched off the pavement as they took off way too quickly for the car's tires.

Susan Morris said to Donny, "He seems like a nice young man but, I never would picture Valerie with someone like that." And from his mother's thoughts, Donny got: *My God, I wonder if his family's connected to the mafia. I hope Val knows what she's doing?*

Donny said, "We need to cut him some slack because of the way Val feels about him, mom. He was probably intimidated by all the questions. I will agree, though, that he's really not the type I picture with her ... a little rough around the edges."

Rose chimed in, "Hey, he may have a heart of gold beneath that tough exterior. Obviously Val sees something she likes there. You shouldn't judge him until you get to know him, right Donny?" But Donny read Rose's thoughts and got: *She probably likes screwing him. There was something in her eyes. She's hooked.*

"Rose is right dear," his mom said.

Donny shrugged his shoulders and asked Rose if she was ready to go. She said yes and they were off to the beach.

As they took off in Tony's car, he said to Val, "Jesus, I'm glad that's over. Your mother and brother are pretty nosy. Can't wait to meet your father."

"Dad's okay. You'll like him. I don't know if he'll like you though ... you're not a doctor or a lawyer. He won't be thrilled about how your dad makes a living," Rose noted.

Tony said, "I really don't give a shit. You're the only one in that family I care about. As long as you and I can climb into bed and rock the room all night, I'm good."

"My Italian stallion," Val laughed as she put her head on his shoulder.

Carla hadn't quite figured him out. After all, it was impossible, right? No one can really read minds can they? But Carla was on the right track.

She was definitely beginning to think that there was something special about Donny … and she wasn't letting go of that idea. Nope, he just didn't seem ordinary to her at all.

She was getting ready to stop by my house that night. No, nothing was going on between us. She was actually coming over to meet Rob. I'd been having these poker games every Thursday for the last few weeks. It was kind of a summer tradition. This year it was my turn to host. Carla didn't play but Rob did. The usual crew was Donny and me and three other guys from school. On that Thursday all of the other three guys couldn't make it for one reason or another. I bumped into Mitch and invited him. He asked if he could bring Rob. I said fine. We needed at least one more player. I remembered this guy Drew Marks, who worked as a waiter at Angelo's for the summer, had asked if I ever needed more players. I'd told him that everyone pretty much shows up but that I'd call him if we needed him. I called him and he was glad to come that night... so we had five players.

Rob had asked Carla to come and meet him at 10:30 p.m. but she came by around 10:00. Actually, I think she just wanted to get to see if Donny was doing his thing. By the time she stopped by Donny had accumulated a big pile of chips. Of course we weren't playing for a lot of money but still, Donny was kicking everyone's ass. I wasn't real sure how I felt about it. I mean obviously I knew that he could read everyone else's thoughts -- a huge advantage when you're playing poker. He knew what people's cards were as soon as they looked at them. He knew exactly when someone was bluffing and when they weren't. It really was no contest. But Donny really didn't care about the money. No, he didn't particularly want to take everyone's cash. He was just playing for the fun of it … for the art of it. He was practicing using his skill to make strategic moves that would win hands and he was enjoying himself immensely. Actually, I was a little surprised no one said anything about how well he was doing beyond the typical, "Man, you're really getting the cards tonight," comments.

When Carla arrived she stood behind Rob, who wasn't particularly happy about losing so badly. "Wow," Carla chided Rob, "looks like I'm gonna have to lend you money to take me out tomorrow night."

"Nah, Morris here is just having a lucky streak. All streaks end … right Donny?" Was it a rhetorical question? If so everyone but Donny and I would be surprised at the answer.

"Just deal 'em, Rob. We'll see," Donny said. Donny sounded a lot different when he was confident.

Rob dealt the cards out … two down cards to everyone as the Texas Holdem' hand began. Drew bet and everyone called him. Rob dealt the flop. It was two fives and a nine. All were different suits. Rob bet heavily and Drew and I folded. Donny and Mitch called him. Rob dealt the turn and it was a seven. Rob bet heavily again and this time Mitch folded. Donny raised Rob a big stack of chips. He knew Rob's two down-cards were a deuce and a four. Three of the cards on the table were hearts and there was only the river left to be dealt. Donny was holding a seven and an eight. So he'd have a minimum of a pair of sevens and, if the river happened to be a six, he would have a straight. Rob called Donny's raise and raised him again.

Donny said, "I'm not buying it Rob. I call you." Donny pushed his chips into the center of the table.

Rob dealt the river and it was a King. Donny focused on Rob's thoughts and got: *Okay buddy you don't have squat do ya? I'll go all in and that'll make you think I'm holding some good cards. You can't tell if I'm bluffing can you? You'll fold. I know you'll fold.*

Rob held his cards close and stared at Donny. Donny just smiled at him and looked up at Carla. She was watching Donny's face. He looked like he already had won.

Donny said, "Check." He wanted Rob to feel confident and make a big bet. Rob looked at his cards, looked up and smiled. Then he said, "All in, Donny-boy. C'mon, go for it." With that he pushed all of his remaining chips to the center of the table. Donny thought for a second, "Am I really going to do this? I know exactly what's in his hand and I'm gonna take his money? Is that why I was given this ability?" He knew what the right thing to do might have been but, after all, he was playing poker to win. His gift was part of him now. You play poker with Donny Morris, that's what you've got to contend with, right? Right.

He looked up at Carla again and smiled. Then he pushed all of his chips into the center of the table and said to Rob, "Sorry man, you're bluffing aren't you?"

Rob threw his cards over a little harder than he should have to show he had nothing.

Donny flipped his cards over to reveal his seven. "Sevens and fives - two pair, buddy. Sorry." Donny reached out with both hands to pull the pot toward him.

Rob wasn't as pissed as he was embarrassed because Carla was standing behind him watching him lose helplessly to Donny Morris. He got up, grabbed Carla by the hand, and mumbled some quick goodbyes as they walked out the door.

I said, "Wow. He wasn't a happy camper was he?"

"Just a sore loser because his girlfriend was here," Mitch said. "He's been like that all his life. He'll get over it."

Outside, Carla took the moment to rub Rob's face in it a little. "You didn't fool him. He knew you were bluffing all along."

"He was just lucky. Christ!" He spat.

Carla didn't say anything but she realized that Donny, again, demonstrated that there was something special about him. You couldn't fool him. It was like he knew what Rob was thinking.

Ever since Sue Fagin's party I've been thinking about whether or not to ask her out on a date. I liked her and I was impressed with how she handled the situation at her party. When I mentioned taking Sue out to Donny he laughed. "She thinks you're cute," he said, "She was thinking that when she first met you at her party. I forgot to tell you."

"Thanks a lot, buddy. A good-looking girl thinks good things about me and you forget to tell me? You're slipping."

"Sorry. I've just had a lot on my mind, lately … like the rest of the world's thoughts, you know?"

"I can't even imagine what that must be like." I replied.

I wanted to talk to Donny about something else … about his gift. It had the potential to be a touchy conversation and I guess I just wasn't real sure I wanted to have it right then and there. But I said, "So, Donny, you've had this magical ability for a little while now, and you've used it to accomplish several different things. What do you think about it? Are you making any rules for yourself? You know, how are you planning on using it?"

Donny thought for a second then he said, "I'm having trouble figuring that out right now, Joey. This whole thing is so new it just absolutely amazes me. I can't believe it's happening to me … but it is. I don't know, when I hear people like my family or you or Rose think things, I almost feel like I'm doing something wrong … invading your private thoughts and hearing stuff I shouldn't. And I'm afraid I'm going to hear things I'll regret hearing. I mean I've already heard my parents think some stuff about each other I'd like to forget. So it's very strange that way. But there are other times, like being able to give my mom advice at the auction, like helping prevent trouble at Sue's party, and like winning money from that jerk, Rob, that make me really, really happy this has happened to me."

"So?" I asked, "What're you gonna do?"

"Jeez, Joey, I mean I can't solve world hunger or prevent war or become King of the United States, can I? I haven't figured out how having this ability can do THAT much good for mankind. And, after all, there are other psychic people in the world, right? People that probably can read minds exist … at least now I think they do. So where are they? What are they doing to save the world? That's where you're going with this, right Joey? You think I should put my power to use to save mankind or something."

"No Donny, that's not what I'm saying at all. I don't think this power, in your 17-year-old body, is going to rock the earth. But, I also wonder if you will put it to good use or if you'll use it for selfish reasons. Don't take that the wrong way but I can definitely see ways you unfairly screw people using your power."

"What … so you think I'd just get into one poker game after another and bleed everyone dry? Or maybe I'll get on a quiz show and read the host's mind as he or the other contestant looks at the questions? Well you know what? I might do either of those. Why not? When that old Shaman, or whatever he was, gave me this gift he never said there was nothing in it for me. There are no rules I know about on how to use it … what to do and what not to do. He just made some vague suggestions. I could tell the world about it and maybe become famous … if I wanted my life to be some kind of freak show. You know, Joey, I just don't know what to do with it yet. It's still new. And by the way, I don't know if I told you this or not, but when Kwajeh gave me this power he said a few things … he didn't just say, 'pouf, you can read minds.' He said I should put the gift to good use. I should help people make their lives better. He also said it may not be permanent and that after, like, three or four months I may have to choose to give it up or keep it. And if I decide to keep it there will be a cost to me. Yeah, that was it. A little scary, no?"

"A little scary, yes." I said. "You didn't really tell me they suggested you use it for good things. You also didn't tell me you might only have it for a few months … and that there would be consequences if you keep it. What do you think that means?"

"I don't know. That was all they said. I mean they did say it is supposed to be used for good but there was no mention of any kind of punishment or consequence if I don't," Donny postulated.

"It's weird, man. What do you think would happen if you used it to steal money or hurt someone?"

Donny replied, "I don't know. They didn't say." In a way, in the poker game, he already did use it to steal money.

I said, "Well, so far you helped your mom, stopped a robbery, and won a card-game. Some noble, some not so much, but nothing earth shattering, and you've only had this for a few days. I'm kind of glad this is you, not me. I mean it'd be amazing to have the power but, somehow, underneath it all, I think it's about good and evil and this thing is meant to be used for good. That's my two cents." I was done.

Donny looked down and said, "I just hope I do the right thing here. It's hard. It's a lot of power and I'm very tempted to show it off. As it is people are beginning to think I'm like, the King of Intuition. I suppose it could be worse."

"You'll figure it out," I said. But I really wasn't sure that would ever happen.

"Hello," came the girl's voice at the end of the phone.

"Hi, Sue?" I said into the receiver.

"Yes, who's this?"

"Joey … Evers. You know, from your party."

"Oh, hi Joey. How are you?"

"Just fine, Sue. Looks like everything turned out okay at the party, right? No bad aftereffects?"

"Oh no. As a matter of fact, even with the problem we had, most people told me they had a really good time. Didn't you?"

"Sure. I mean, the whole thing was kind of strange but I guess we were lucky that Donny was paying attention and that you acted quickly. I thought it was a better party when it got smaller and moved inside anyway."

"Yeah, that's what most people said," she replied.

This was always the hard part for me. "So I was thinking that maybe you and I could get together sometime. We could go to a concert, a movie, the beach, whatever you'd like … or we could just sit around and talk if you want."

"Okay," she said quickly, "It doesn't matter what we do but I like the idea of talking … we should get to know each other better."

With the hard part over, I said, "How's tomorrow night? I could pick you up at seven and, if the weather's okay maybe we'll just head down to the beach, put out a blanket, bring some drinks, and we'll talk. How does that sound?"

"Good! I'll see you tomorrow."

We both hung up and I dialed Donny immediately to tell him about my date with Sue.

"Hello," Valerie Morris said.

"Hi Val, it's Joey, is Donny around?"

"He just left. He went over to Rose's but said you could call him there if you want."

I said thanks and hung up. It might have been my imagination but it seemed to me Donny was spending a bit more one-on-one time with Rose. It kind of worried me. I just didn't want Rose to get hurt, and the more time she spent alone with Donny, I think the greater the chance of Rose getting hurt. I dialed Rose's number and got her on the first ring. I said hi and asked to speak to Donny for a moment.

"Hey Joey, what's up?" He said.

"I just called Sue Fagin and asked her out. We're going to the beach tomorrow night."

"Cool," he said. "You want me and Rose to come along for support?"

"You're kidding, right? This is my first date with a pretty girl. Why would I want you and Rose hanging around. Besides, because the three of us are such good friends, it would probably make Sue uncomfortable. Just wanted to let you know what's going on," I said.

"Great, man. I'm happy for you. Let me know how it goes. Bye."

The next morning I got to the gym late (it was after 8:30) and most of the stationary bikes were taken. So I thought I'd start with a treadmill. Before I could climb up on the one I'd picked out Carla tapped me on the shoulder.

"Hey, Carla. Are you here every day?" I asked.

"Just about Evers. You seem to be doing a lot of work on yourself too."

"So what's up with you Carla?" I wanted to get on the treadmill

"Well," she said slowly, "Rob and I are done."

I did a slight double take. "Done? As in broken up? What happened?" I was surprised.

"I guess I just got bored with Rob's 'I'm a big jock' mentality. I couldn't stand it anymore so I broke up with him."

"How'd he take it?" I asked. But I really wasn't that concerned.

"He was pissed for a while … but he'll get over it. There are plenty of fish out there in the sea."

"Yeah, I suppose so," I said, "so now what're you gonna do?"

"I don't know. It's not like I won't get asked out. It's just that all the guys know I've been with Rob for a while so they've stopped asking. I'm hoping when the word gets out I'll get some new invitations. What do you think?"

"What do I think? I think you'll be fine. You don't seem like the type to worry about it."

"I'm not. What're you up to?" She asked.

"Not much. Got a first date tonight though, with Sue Fagin."

A grin spread across Carla's face, "Sue Fagin huh? I think she's great, Joey. The two of you may hit if off real well. What's that going to do to your little threesome?" Was that her way of asking about Donny, I wondered?

"Nothing. Donny and Rose and I always have been friends. No reason to believe my dating Sue would change anything. Besides, it's only my first date."

"So Donny and Rose aren't really anything more than friends."

"I told you, Banes, the three of us have been friends for years. That's it. I gotta' get going here. Need to put in some time on this treadmill."

"Okay, don't let me hold you up. Just giving you my news. Say hello to Donny," she said as she walked away.

I scratched my head as I mulled the possibility that Carla wanted to get together with Donny.

Chapter Ten

When I got home from the gym I called Donny.

"Hey my man, I've got some interesting news for you." I trumpeted.

"And what would that be?" Donny replied.

"I just came from the gym. Carla told me she dumped Rob."

"Really!" Donny exclaimed, the excitement obvious in his voice.

"Yes, looks like it just happened. She was bored and tired of Rob. And, well, I think she might be open to getting to know YOU better."

There was quiet on the other end of the phone. I waited, finally he said, "Why would you say that?" I told him about the conversation I'd had with Carla and how she'd watched him at the party and then at the card game. I also told him about Carla's mother's feedback from the auction.

"Bottom line here Donny, Carla thinks there may be something special about you. She couldn't quite put her finger on it but she even said to me something like, 'It's almost like he reads minds.' Really."

"Jesus," Donny croaked, "I don't know what to say. Would she go out with me on a date?" He asked.

"Of course, dumbo. Why do you think she's been asking about you?"

"That's … incredible. I'd really be nervous, I think. But … I should ask her, right? I mean, should I wait a while so Rob doesn't totally flip out?"

"I can't see why?" I offered, "She's broken up and free. You're free. Why wait? Besides, you'll know what she's thinking every step of the way, won't you?"

"Oh, I don't think I'd be able to just keep listening to everything she's thinking. What kind of relationship would that be?" But, inside, Donny wasn't sure what he'd do.

"A safe one," I said.

Donny said, "I'll think about it. But, thanks Joey, that's great news. Maybe I'll call Rose and ask her what she thinks. She's a chick. She ought to know what Carla's going through."

"Donny, be careful. You already know Rose has feelings for you. If you talk about taking Carla out with Rose, you might hurt her feelings and make her jealous." I suggested.

"Hmm. I'll think about that one too. You still going out with Sue Fagin tonight?"

"Far as I know." I said.

"Well have a good time. Tell me about it tomorrow. See ya." He hung up.

"Hey Tony … what' going on?" Was the greeting Tony Donato got from Louie Fiero as he walked into Louie's office above the grocery store.

Tony just shrugged.

"So, everything good with you this week, Tony?" Louie asked from behind his antique oak desk.

"Yeah, yeah, everything's fine," he said as he reached into the inner pocket of his sports jacket and pulled out the envelope. He handed it across the desk to the big man whose outstretched arm had a gold watch the size of an apple strapped to it. Louie opened the envelope, pulled out the money, and counted the bills one by one by laying them out on his desk.

"All here, Tony. Your father will be proud of you. Any of the clients give you trouble?"

"No Louie, everything went fine. Everyone cooperates … mostly because they're scared shitless not to." Tony said.

"That's good, Tony. Hey, I may have another job for you. It'll be a little bit bigger than the last one but, of course, the money will be better too," he laughed.

"What kind of job, Louie?"

"I'll let you know when the time comes. In the mean time just keep collecting from your regular customers. I'll see you next week, okay?"

"Yeah, fine Louie. See ya," Tony said as he opened the door and left.

As he was walking down the stairs to the street Tony thought to himself, "When's my dad gonna let me do something really big? Something that'll make me some real money. I hate this little collection crap. It's for morons and I'm definitely not a moron."

Tony would've talked about it directly with his dad except his dad, Rocco Donato, had one basic rule regarding Tony: No talking about business with his family. All Tony had, for now, was big Louie.

There was no doubt about it in his mind. It was Donny's time to ask Carla out on a date. But what would happen when Rose found out about it. No matter how he looked at it, it would be less painful for her if she found out about it from him. He was convinced he'd have to tell Rose himself. He was going to call her, but then he thought it would be much better if he actually knew what she was really thinking so he decided to tell her in person. He called her and asked if he could come over and talk to her. She said she'd only have a few minutes but, if he hurried, she'd be okay.

When he got to her house she was sitting on her front porch. He walked up and said hi. She was anxious to know what was so important that he had to see her in person.

"It's not that it's so important, but I really wanted to see if you could give me some advice." Donny said.

"About what?" She asked.

"Joey told me that Carla broke up with Rob. It shouldn't be a shock for me to tell you I want to ask her out and, well, I'd like any advice you might want to give me because I value your opinion," he said carefully.

Rose turned a little red. Donny immediately got: *Shit. I was afraid that bimbo would get tired of her Ken doll and the minute she let go Donny's gonna take a stupid plunge.*

Rose thought for a moment and said, "Donny, you know Carla is a snob and, basically, an airhead, right? I mean what could you hope to get out of a relationship with someone like that?"

"Rose, I know you don't particularly like her but consider how I feel. I've had a crush on her for a long time and I don't want to blow this. Can't you be objective and tell me what you think I should do?" He asked.

"Yes," she said, "Here's what to do. DON'T DO IT. She's going to be bad for you. She uses people to get whatever it is she wants and then she drops them. If she would dump Rob Talbot that easily, what chance do you think you would possibly have?"

"Okay. I can see you hate her and I'm not going to get any words of wisdom from you about her. I guess I'm on my own here. Well, don't be surprised when I ask her out, okay?"

"Okay dummy. But you are really asking for trouble here. This isn't going to make you happy at all."

"Well look," Donny said, "this can't be allowed to affect our friend-ship, right?"

"I don't know Donny. You hang around with her all the time and there'll be very little time for us. I guess we'll see." She huffed. And she thought: *What can I possibly do to make this not happen? He's going to fall for her like a ton of bricks. I can't believe it.* Donny was tuned into her and heard. He really didn't want to lose Rose's friendship. She was important to him. But, he wasn't sure she was as important as being with Carla.

I was so looking forward to taking Sue Fagin out that I arrived at her house ten minutes early for our date. I thought about staying in the car for a while but that seemed stupid, so I got out and rang the bell. Sue answered the bell like her ear was glued to the door. She seemed happy to see me.

"Hi. I'm a little early" I said.

"Yeah, that's fine. You wanna come in or just take off to the beach?" Sue offered.

"Since I've seen your house at the party why don't we just get going?"

We got in the car and drove off toward Lake Monroe beach. It was twilight and the colors in the sky made me think of art class - red, orange, violet, blue, yellow and pink. Somehow it seemed right for an outdoor date with Sue Fagin.

On the way to the beach Sue told me all about her family and how her grandparents had moved here from Ireland. Her grandpa was a salesman because he didn't have a trade and he didn't seem to be able to keep a job for very long. Sue's dad was an only child and he became a star student at school. When he went to Dartmouth College on a scholarship he became the pride of the family. Three years at Columbia law prepared him to open what was now the most prestigious law practice in the county. Sue, and her sister, Donna had lived in their house for their entire lives.

We both thought it was funny that Lake Monroe was where we'd both grown up and yet we sort of knew who each other was from school but we had never actually met. I was amazed that I hadn't known this girl with the huge blue eyes and the sweet, round face. And, as the evening went on I grew more and more excited about her. We just seemed to be a natural fit in many ways. I really liked the way her eyes sparkled when I talked to her. She was really listening to me. I liked the way she walked, and laughed, and dressed. In fact, there wasn't much I didn't like. I hate saying it but I really think I fell for her in less than an hour. The cool thing though, was I felt exactly the same feelings coming back from her. She liked to touch my arm and she sat close to me when she could. She looked into my eyes when we talked and she laughed at my jokes. My God, a girl that laughed at my jokes. Could life be any better?

Sue and I sat on the blanket and talked for hours. It didn't matter what the subject was. We just liked talking to each other. As it started to get cooler, I felt very comfortable putting my arm around her to keep her warm. She was grateful. She smelled so good I wanted to touch her skin, so I asked her if I could. She smiled and nodded and I reach my hand out and touched her cheek. She actually closed her eyes and blushed a little but I couldn't have been happier. Her skin felt like a newborn baby and I didn't want to stop. But I did. I told her that I couldn't believe how adorable she was and that I've never had anything like this happen to me on a first date. She said that she had noticed me at the party and knew there was a connection. She had hoped I would call her and she said she was really happy I did. My hormones were on fire and I couldn't help myself. I leaned over very close to her face and asked if I could kiss her. Without saying anything, she looked up at me for a second, closed her eyes, and brought her silky lips to mine. We put our arms around each other and kissed for a long time. Her mouth was warm and soft and wet and I just couldn't get enough. I don't think either one of us knew what to say so we let the kisses speak for us. It was fantastic.

When we decided it was time to go home we were both kind of sad. The car ride back to her house was quiet. We were holding hands while I drove and Sue just looked content. When we got to her house I walked her to the door.

I said, "Sue, this was the best time I've had with anyone I can remember. You're just so easy to be with, so easy to talk to. It's really incredible."

She put her arms around my waist and said, "We don't want to move too fast here, Joey, but I feel the very same way. You are a wonderful guy and for me to know that on one date must mean you are very special. I've gotta' go. Call me," she said as we moved together for a long good-night kiss. I watched her put the key in the door, open it, and close it behind her. As I climbed into my car and drove home I know I had a smile on my face. Who would have expected this to happen? Me and Sue Fagin. Boom! Like out of nowhere. I couldn't wait to tell Donny.

Donny was nervous about this phone call. He wasn't sure he knew what to say to Carla, but nothing was going to stop him.

He picked up the receiver and dialed her number. It rang four times and he almost hung up. "Hello," said Carla's mother, Elaine.

"Hello, Mrs. Banes. This is Donny Evers. We met at the antique auction last week. Remember me?"

"Oh yes, Donny. How are you?"

"I'm fine thanks. Um, is Carla home?"

"Yes she is. I'll tell her you're calling," she said.

After what seemed like a week, Carla's voice came through the phone.

"Hello, Donny?"

"Yeah, it's me, Carla. How're you doin'?" He said kind of shakily.

"I'm good. What's going on with you?"

"Well, I heard you and Rob were no longer seeing each other. Sorry about that, I guess. I thought that maybe you and I could go out, y'know, have dinner or see a movie or something like that?" He was really uncomfortable but was trying to maintain himself.

"Hmm," she said, "dinner or a movie, huh? I guess so. I mean, I'm free to go and do whatever I want now. Sure."

Donny was happy that part was over with, "Okay, how's Friday night? We can talk earlier and I'll pick you up for dinner at 6:30. Sound okay?" he asked.

Carla paused. She didn't make anything easy. Then finally, "Yeah, okay. Call me late afternoon when you've figured out the details. See you then. Bye." She hung up.

Donny put down the phone and let out a deep breath of air. He was finally going out with Carla Banes - his dream girl. He could hardly wait.

I went over to Donny's house the morning after my date with Sue. I couldn't wait to tell him about it. When I got there I found him in his room. He said, "So, how was the big night." He immediately got: *I can't even believe how much I like this girl. It's like I'm in love with her after one date. I can't wait to see her again. I'll have to call her later.*

"I had a really good time," I said.

He replied, laughing, "Apparently that's a huge understatement. You're thinking you love her?"

I was flustered and reminded myself that I didn't like it when Donny read my thoughts. "It was special, Donny. She and I just seemed like we were perfect for each other. I can't wait to see her again," I gushed.

"I can see that. And I can hear that. Fantastic! That's great for you. You deserve something much more than having to hang around Rose and me all the time," he said. And then, "Speaking of getting something more than you deserve, guess who's going out with Carla on Friday?"

I smiled at him because I knew how much he wanted this, "Really! That's excellent Donny. You're finally getting your chance. The only thing I'd say is you need to be very careful with her. She already thinks you may be some kind of psychic. I don't think it'd be a good thing if she found out you have real telepathic power."

"Don't worry about it, Joey. She'll never know … and I'll always have the advantage of knowing what she's thinking." He smiled. But I wasn't crazy about that idea either. Something just didn't seem right about it.

I stayed for a while and then I left. It was hard not to think about Sue. I really liked her.

A few miles away, Rose was sitting in a chair in her living room staring out the window. It had just started to rain and that added to her glum mood. She was really upset about Donny asking Carla out. Of course, Carla could always say no. Rose didn't know yet that Carla and Donny were going out Friday. Rose knew that I was going out with Sue Fagin. I don't think she liked that either. It kind of left Rose alone. In her mind, one minute she and I and Donny were good friends spending all of our time together, and the next, well, Donny would be with Carla and I'd be with Sue. I don't blaming her for being upset. It was like she was losing her best friends. Rose thought that she needed to do some things differently. She thought maybe a kind of new beginning for her would help. As she looked in the mirror at her curly blond hair, freckles, and brown eyes, she was unhappy. She wanted to look different. She thought she needed to be more attractive. She decided that there were a few steps she would take. First, she would straighten her hair. She'd had the curls since she was a little girl and now she wanted to grow up. Next, she would quickly learn how to wear makeup so she wouldn't just look like a mass of freckles every day. Third, she would go to the gym and work on her body. She could build herself up so she wouldn't look like a little boy. Lastly, she would need to buy some more stylish, more feminine clothes, to accentuate the new curves she was planning on having. Yep, that was it. She'd make herself over into the new Rose, someone who was desirable and had sex appeal. Poor Rose, she didn't see the beauty that was already there, but, I guess if nobody tells you you're pretty you may never know.

Chapter Eleven

Donny was right on time for his first date with Carla. He felt a little nervous and his palms were sweaty. They'd talked that afternoon and decided on a local Chinese restaurant, Soo-Ling. When Donny rang the bell Elaine Banes let him in and led him to the living room. She offered him a drink and said Carla should be down in a minute. Donny sat there for 20 minutes, waiting patiently, before Carla appeared. She looked terrific of course! Something about her long black hair and piercing green eyes got Donny going. He was also captivated by her figure, in particular the long legs. There wasn't much not to like in the way Carla looked.

They said goodbye to Mrs. Banes and left. Donny opened up his mind as they got into his car. He got: *What is this piece of junk? A Pontiac? A Buick? Looks really old.*

So he said, "This is actually my mom's other car. I'm getting a new one soon. Probably when we go back to school in the fall." He lied.

"Oh that's nice, Donny." She said. Donny got: *Who cares?*

"So Carla … what happened between you and Rob? Can you talk about it or would you rather not?" Donny asked.

"No big deal. Actually our time together got boring and I just didn't want to do it anymore. You know how that goes, right?"

"Right."

"But I don't want to talk about me. Let's talk about you," she said. "That was pretty smart the way you handled that scene at Sue Fagin's party. I heard it was your idea to just say a neighbor called the cops. Is that right? How did you know those two guys were planning on robbing the place … and they had a knife?" She was full of questions.

"Yes, it was my idea. I just thought that would be good enough to scare them away ... and, fortunately, it was. I, uh, overheard them talking out back and it just sounded to me like bad stuff was going to happen. I never actually saw the knife but I knew the guy had it." Donny said. He didn't mean to say that last part but it kind of slipped out.

"You knew the guy had it? How?" She asked.

"I, uh, think I heard him mention it to his friend." Donny said unconvincingly.

"Uh huh. Well that was something, Donny. I've gotta' tell you that my mom thinks you're psychic. She was sitting behind you guys at that auction and she says it was as if you knew what everyone was thinking before they said it. She thought you were amazing."

"No big deal. I've been going there with my mother a long time. You sort of get to understand how people bid after a while." He said.

"But, also at the card game. You kicked everyone's ass. They all said you were immune to bluffs. I saw it myself. It was like you knew what Rob and the others were thinking. Are you some kind of psychic, Donny? Because, I believe in psychic powers even though I haven't met anyone that actually has them. It's just one of those things you know is out there. What do you think?"

Donny thought, "Wow ... she's really into the psychic thing wholehog. She's asking if I'm a psychic. That's incredible and a little scary." Amazing himself, Donny was half tempted to tell her about the Incident but he caught himself. He knew he would have just been showing off ... not a good idea.

He said, "Um, am I psychic? No I don't think I'm psychic. Do I believe people can be? Yes. I think I'm just good at figuring out what people want and how their minds work. My mother thinks I'm just very intuitive. I get that from some of my other friends, too."

Carla said, "Well I think that's a fantastic quality to have. Just look at the advantage you have dealing with other people. It's like you practically know what they're thinking," Donny thought, "It's because I DO know what they're thinking."

They got to the restaurant and were seated in a booth near the back of the restaurant. Donny had swung the conversation away from things psychic to school, relationships, popular movies, politics, parents, college choices and the like. Carla, however, still seemed fascinated with Donny's intuition. She took every opportunity to come back to it. It was hard for Donny because he had just been getting used to being open about it with me. When he heard someone's thoughts that mattered he wanted to say something about them or do something about them. So, as much as he really wanted to show-off for his dream girl, he had to be careful.

When the waiter took their order, Carla ordered the Peking duck and asked if it had MSG. The Chinese-American waiter replied, "No MSG." But Donny knew differently. He couldn't help himself, "The Peking duck has MSG in it" he blurted out. The waiter said, "No, no it doesn't," but he was thinking it did. So Donny said to a surprised Carla, "Order something else if you don't want MSG." Carla just stared at him with a look of disbelief on her face. "No, you know what, I'm gonna have the Peking duck." Donny shrugged but when the waiter left he said, "I'm telling you, it's going to have MSG in it. You shouldn't have ordered it." Carla said, "That's exactly the point. I'll know from the minute I taste it if it has MSG. I just want to see if that waiter lied to me." But she was also thinking she'd check on how good Donny's "intuition" was as well.

When the waiter brought out the food Carla was anxious to taste it. She took one bit and said, "I'll be damned, MSG, sure as hell." They called for the waiter, sent back the duck and ordered Pork Lo Mein, after Carla gave him a piece of her mind for telling her there was no MSG in the duck.

Carla said, "You going to tell me what that was about? I mean how on earth did you know he was lying?"

"No big deal. I just think the waiter was wrong," he said innocently.

"But how would you know?" Carla asked.

Donny was grasping for straws now, "I remember from the last time I was here. Someone ordered the Peking duck and didn't feel well from the MSG. No big deal."

Carla said, "Right. You remembered from last time. You are incred-ible. I think you just, somehow, knew that guy was not telling the truth. Isn't that what happened?" She was relentless.

"Nope. I remembered from last time and didn't want to see you get sick." He stuck to his guns.

They finished dinner and got back into the car.

Donny said, "What would you like to do now?"

Carla replied, "My parents are out. Wanna' come over and we'll listen to music or watch a movie?"

He thought that sounded fine so they stopped at a video store, rented a few movies and drove back to Carla's house.

Donny felt funny being alone with Carla in her living room. She was much more a woman than a girl and Donny had only been with girls. He was paying careful attention with his mind though. On one hand he didn't want to cheat and possibly screw up their relationship before it had any chance of being something. On the other hand he wanted to know what she was thinking so he wouldn't make any big mistakes.

When Carla put on the movie and turned some of the lights off Donny started to feel a little more comfortable. He tuned her in for a minute and got some unimportant thoughts that had nothing to do with him. Then all of a sudden: *I wonder if Donny-boy is gonna make a move on me tonight. Maybe it's too early - first date and all. If he does, though, I'm not gonna let him do anything. Just a good-night kiss. He likes me. He'll be back ... and I've got to find out more about that incredible mind of his.*

So Donny knew exactly what not to do. They sat together on the couch till the movie was over. They talked about unimportant stuff for a while and he got up to leave. They walked to the door and she said, "I had a nice time, Donny. Sorry about the third degree but that intuition of yours really amazes me. Tell me, what am I thinking right now?" Donny tuned in and knew she was thinking: Gimme a kiss, Donny-boy. He smiled and said, "Well of course it's time for a good-night kiss, right?" He got mad at himself because it was too easy ... but it was also obvious. No great-sounding mental feat. Carla smiled and said, "Right you are." She leaned over and kissed him. It was awkward for Donny but the idea of Carla Banes' kissing him was just unbelievable to him. He put his arms around her and pulled her closer. She stayed for a second but then moved backward.

Donny said, "Can I call you again?"

She said, "Sure. Good night Donny." Donny wasn't really thrilled to hear her think: *Hmm, bet he's got a boner.* He got into his car and went home.

Over the next few weeks I saw Sue almost every day. I was crazy about that girl and I know she felt the same for me. It really changed my life because I barely had time to see Rose anymore, and Donny had started to spend time with Carla. Yep, his dream began to come true. I called Rose every few days and I even started to see her showing up at the same gym as Carla and I. She was changing. Her hair was straight and long and a new, more attractive golden color. The old dirty blond curls from her childhood were gone. Her face looked different too. I think it was because she'd started wearing makeup every day, something she never did before. It smoothed out her skin, accentuated the shape of her cheekbones, hid her freckles and brought out those smiling eyes. She also was dressing differently. She had, outfits now. You didn't see her very often in jeans and a T-shirt. If she wore jeans, now they were mostly designer jeans, with some kind of tight stretchy top. Rose was growing into a very attractive woman and guys were beginning to notice.

Because we'd found each other, Sue and I were having a great summer. We'd go to the beach a few times a week. Once or twice Donny and Carla came with us and, that was when I first became nervous about Carla's influence on Donny.

Donny was different around Carla. It was like she was the boss and Donny was there to please her. I'm not exactly surprised that this is the way their relationship developed, but it bothered me to see him like that. Also, and maybe more disturbing, Carla seemed to know about Donny's gift. It's not like he told her (and he promised me that, at least at that point, he hadn't) but she knew. She just knew from the way he reacted to people, and to her. He knew what they were thinking and she knew it. And then the business with the casino started.

Carla had a friend whose boyfriend could get fake ID's. For $200 he'd take your picture and, in about two weeks, come back to you with a NY state driver's license that looked just like the real thing. They were supposed to be as close to the real thing as you could buy. Carla had one and she wanted to get one for Donny so they could go to the casino that just opened on an Indian reservation upstate. Donny was nervous about it and I think he knew Carla wanted to push him into gambling for her. He resisted. But, after Carla slept with Donny he seemed to lose all will of his own. He was hers. She arranged to get him the fake ID. I felt really bad for him. I mean, here's a kid that had a telepathic gift that was so special he was one of a kind. I'm sure he could have found ways to put it to the use the Shaman had probably intended when he gave it to him, but Donny was too caught up in pleasing Carla to focus on that.

I dropped over to Donny's one day in late July to talk to him. I found him out in his backyard listening to the radio.

"Hi buddy. Haven't seen you in a few days so I thought I'd stop by." I said.

"Hi," is all he said.

"Uh, something the matter, Donny? That wasn't exactly an enthusiastic hello."

"No. Just thinking about some things." He said drearily.

"Wanna' talk about them? This is me, Donny."

"Not really, Joey. But I think I made a mistake." He said.

"Uh oh," I said. "What kind of mistake are we talking about?

"I know I said I wouldn't but I told Carla the story about the Incident and my telepathy two nights ago."

I choked a little, "Oh no, Donny! Why the hell would you do that? I mean she was just guessing that you were very intuitive. You shouldn't have told her. Now you have no idea who she'll tell."

"Yeah, I know. But first of all, she somehow pretty much guessed that I had some kind of special power. I'm pretty sure that's what she likes about me to begin with. And second, I don't think she totally believed me about

Kenworth Park and Kwajeh. Besides, if she told anyone, who would believe her?" He said.

I thought for a minute, then, "I don't know, Donny. You've only been dating her a few weeks and you suspect she only likes you for your ability to read people's minds? What if she wants you to do stuff with your power for her?"

"I'm not worried about it really," he said, "I'm in control of what I do. I don't have to do anything I don't want to do, right?"

"Theoretically yeah, but Carla can be pretty convincing. Does she know I know about your power?"

"Yes. I told her. But she swore on her life that she'd never say anything to anyone else. Besides, I haven't really done much with my so-called gift since I've had it. So it's really not been that big a deal."

"Fine," I said, but I was really disappointed that Donny did this.

"Donny, have you thought about the fact that school begins again in a few weeks. It's right around the corner. Having the power to read minds in school will put you on a new level. It's a little scary."

"I'm not going to think about it until I get there. I've got a lot to think about as is," he complained.

"Just promise me you won't do anything stupid. I know you and Carla are going to the casino soon. That scares me.

Donny said, "Don't worry. No big deal. I'm just gonna go to have some fun."

That didn't make me feel any better, but what could I do about it.

Before I left I said, "Hey, when's the last time you saw Rose?"

He thought for a second and said, "I talked to her last week on the phone but I haven't seen her in a lot longer than that."

"You're gonna be surprised! She's made some changes and she looks terrific. I don't think you'd recognize her."

"Really? The only thing she said to me was that she was spending some more time at the gym."

I said, "Well she is, and when you see her you'll know that it's been time well spent. Gotta' go. Just be careful."

"Yeah." Donny said.

When he got the call, Tony Donato was excited. Louie just said, "We got something bigger for you. It's time to step up. Come see me." But that was all it took. Something bigger. Tony liked the sound of that. After all he deserved something bigger didn't he? He was smart and cool and was going to be a rock star in the family someday, right? So something bigger sounded just about right.

He walked back into the Morris' living room, sat back down on the couch, and put his arm back around Val's shoulder. She leaned over and kissed him.

"What's with people calling you here? And who's Louie?" She asked. She had answered the phone when Louie called.

"He's just a guy that works with my father. They've got a project they want me to work on. I think I may be in line for a promotion." He leaned over and they kissed again. "I could be making some really big bucks in a short period of time. How does that sound?"

"Sounds great if it makes you happy, Tony. You know I don't care that much about money, but if it's important to you it's important to me."

"Well it is. A man's gotta' work and a man's gotta' do the right thing for himself and his family. You're almost my family now, Val. I'm just looking out for our future."

Val thought for a second about marrying Tony. She was only in college but she was crazy about him. She thought anything was possible.

Tony stood up and said, "I gotta' go, Val. I need to check in with this guy Louie and see what's up. I'll call you later, okay?"

She said, "Okay sweetie. Good luck." Tony walked out the door and got into his car.

During that whole summer I always wondered what was happening between Donny and Val and his parents. I mean, how could he live in their house, see them every day, eat meals with them, and not have them discover that he had a new talent for reading minds? It was strange to me, but I guess when you've been together for someone's lifetime, seeing them change isn't startling. And Donny's mom and sister always thought he was a smart, intuitive kid anyway. But I was surprised at some of the daily occurrences in their home surrounding Donny's gift. It just didn't seem like they even wanted to notice his behavior.

There were times that Edward Morris would be standing near the door thinking: *Where are my car keys?* Donny would appear from the other end of the room and say, "If you're looking for your keys, Dad, I saw them in the kitchen." His dad would just say, "Thanks," and he'd go into the kitchen to retrieve them.

Or they'd be having dinner and Donny would hear his mother think: *I want some more potatoes.* Donny would reach for the bowl and just pass it to her without saying anything. What was remarkable was that she didn't flinch when things like that happened. She just took it for granted because he's her son, and he knows her well.

There were a few times I heard about that were really strange but Donny seemed to handle them. Like the time Val and Donny were watching TV with their mother and Donny heard his mother think: *Oh Lord, what is that pain in my side. It keeps coming back. Oh, it's killing me!* Donny turned to his mother and said, "If you are in such great pain why don't we call a doctor or take you to a hospital?"

Val turned around and looked at him and said, "What are you talking about? She didn't say anything about being in pain."

Donny said "Mom, are you not in pain?"

She said "Well yes I am but how ..."

"The look on your face," Donny said. "What else could it be?" Val just looked at him.

Or the time he heard Val think: *I wanna' go away with Tony this weekend but I can't let mom and dad know. They would be pissed.*

Donny said to Val, "If you want to go away with Tony, don't worry about mom and dad. I'll cover for you."

Val's jaw dropped and she said, "Did I say I wanted to go away with Tony?"

Donny realized his mistake and said, "Yes you did. Don't you remember? Not five minutes ago."

Val said, "I don't think so. You are weird, Donny."

Stuff like that happened all the time in Donny's life. But his parents and, to a lesser extent his sister, didn't really know what was going on with him. I don't think they wanted to know.

When Tony got to Louie's office it smelled of cigars. Louie had a big ugly stogie in his mouth and the room was filled with smoke.

"How ya' doin', kid?" Louie said.

"I'm good, Louie. What's up with you?"

"So let me ask you Tony, you ready for something big? Something very important to your family?"

"Absolutely."

"Now, you understand that once you accept this job there's no turning back, there's no changing your mind. And you can't under any circumstances tell anybody, and I mean fuckin' anybody, about it. You understand? Cause if you did the consequences would be huge, okay? Also, if we decide you are

NOT the right guy for this job, or you don't want it, and we give it to some-one else, the same rules hold. You don't EVER tell anyone anything about it. Capiche?"

Tony nodded his head up and down but didn't say anything. He was suddenly becoming a little nervous.

"Your father has been in business a long time. He tries to treat people fairly as a good businessman should. But every once in a while someone takes advantage of a generous man like your father and does something that, well let's just say, something he really shouldn't do. I want to talk to you about the solution."

Forty-five minutes later Tony left Louie's office and got into his car. He put the package Louie had given him under the passenger seat and took a deep breath. He thought he'd made the right decision and he knew what he had to do now.

Four days later the headline in the Lake Monroe Times read:

LINDEN BUSINESSMAN, DAVID FINN, SHOT TO DEATH OUT-SIDE HIS HOME.

People didn't get shot very often in that area. Linden was the next town over from Lake Monroe so this was a big deal.

The article said that David Finn owned a trash collection business and was thought to have ties to organized crime. He was apparently mow-ing his lawn that afternoon when someone got out of a car, walked up to him and put three shots into his head using a .38 caliber handgun with a silencer. The police were asking for information from anyone who might have seen the shooter or the car. They knew how the murder was committed because an elderly lady who lived across the street saw a car stop, a door open, and someone step out. The car blocked her view of the crime but she did hear the three shots and saw the car take off afterwards.

Donny's mom mentioned it at the dinner table the next night.

She said, "It's getting worse and worse with gangsters shooting people in their own front yards. What is going on?"

Donny just nodded his head.

Val said, "It's not so safe out there anymore. You never know who to trust, do you?"

Their guest, Tony, looked up from his plate and said, "Yeah, things are getting worse," and he kept on eating.

Donny was focused on his own thoughts and didn't bother to read anyone else's mind.

The Cuyoga Casino was about an hour and a half away from Lake Monroe. Carla and Donny were on their way for a gambling trip complete with fake ID. The fake New York State driver's licenses only said they were nine months older than they actually were so Donny didn't feel that badly about it. They also had hundreds of dollars that both of them had saved, and an intent on Carla's part at least, to make a killing.

The minute Donny had confirmed that he was indeed some kind of "freak" that could now read minds, Carla was working on ways they could use that for their advantage. She remembered the poker game she'd been at with Rob, and how Donny knew what everyone had in their hands because he could read their thoughts. This would be a piece of cake at a casino, she reasoned, because Donny was just a clean-cut young guy who wouldn't arouse suspicion. Besides no one would be able to nail him for cheating anyway. Carla thought this was perfect. The only weak link was the fake ID, but she didn't think that would be a big deal since 18 was the legal age for gambling in New York … and they were practically there.

Carla was dressed for the occasion. She had chosen a short, tight, black cocktail dress with matching shoes. The heels would've been hard for most girls to walk on but not Carla. She practiced and she was good at it. She'd asked Donny to wear a sport jacket and slacks with decent shoes so he looked respectable and wouldn't attract any undue attention.

When they pulled up to the casino Donny was impressed. A lot of money must have gone into this place. It was huge and it was almost all glass. They had a valet park the car (Carla was pretty much embarrassed each time they went out in that old Buick but Donny kept promising he'd be getting something newer soon).

As they walked through the huge doorway a very large man in a tuxedo stopped them and asked for their identification. They pulled out their licenses and gave them to him. Donny scanned guy's mind as he scrutinized the licenses. The man was reviewing known forgery points like the hologram and the seal. He wasn't the least bit suspicious. Donny even winked at Carla, who smiled. After a few moments the man returned their ID and welcomed them to Cuyoga Casino. They stepped inside.

The interior of the casino was beautiful as well. It had more multi-tiered chandeliers than Donny had ever seen in his life. In front of them there were rows and rows of slot machines of many different kinds. Donny saw signs for jackpots, which went up to $3,000,000. They walked past the slots and into the roulette area. There was table after table with different betting limits. Donny liked roulette because he liked calculating odds but that wasn't why he was here tonight. They stopped at one of the many crap tables to watch people play the game. It was pretty packed and people were getting drunk. A lot of that had to do with the free drinks the short-skirted waitresses kept offering to anyone who was playing.

They walked through a huge archway into a room with even more slot machines. Donny couldn't resist putting a few quarters into the slots just for fun. He didn't win anything. He lost five quarters.

Pretty soon Carla said, "Lets' keep walking. I know there are poker games in here somewhere." So they kept moving toward the back of the huge casino and, through another portal, they found the poker tables.

There were several kinds of poker games available and several different dollar limits. Donny told Carla he wanted to watch for a while to get the feel of the game and try hearing thoughts, so they picked a spot at a $10 Texas Holdem' table behind the players, and they watched.

The particular people at that table seemed to be unspectacular poker players. Donny practiced listening to how they thought and, as he focused on each one individually, he knew exactly what they were holding in their hands and, moments before they did it, he knew just what they were going to do.

But Donny was worried about this. The idea of cheating by reading minds was bad enough. Donny was more concerned that he hadn't been using his power very often for really good things. He was worried that the Shaman would somehow know that he was, in effect, stealing from people and there might be a bad consequence. Yet, he didn't want to disappoint Carla. He was living his dream with her and he wasn't ready for anything to change that so Donny sat down at the table as soon as there was an open seat.

He got $300 in chips to begin with. They had brought $800 between them -- $500 was Donny's. Their plan was to win a few thousand dollars and split all the profits 50-50. That, of course, was Carla's idea ... but Donny didn't care, as long as she was happy.

Donny won the first pot because everyone else folded. He heard each one make the decision in their mind before they actually made the moves out loud. He didn't fall for a bluff on the next hand and won $500. He purposely lost a small amount on the hand after that so it wouldn't look like he couldn't lose. That's how the first half-hour went. Carla stood behind him, rubbing his neck and whispering in his ear the whole time. A waitress was bringing them champagne and Carla kept drinking it. Donny was worried it would mute his telepathic power so he just sipped.

After about an hour at the table, people were commenting on how well Donny was doing. He had about $7,000 in chips and he'd only started with $500. Donny thought it was pretty good work for one night and he asked to cash out. Carla grabbed his neck and said, "What're you doing? You're just warming up."

Donny said, "No, I think I'm done at this table. I don't want to start losing. Let's go." He got up.

But Carla wasn't happy. She was smart enough not to make a scene and attract attention but she wanted to stay. Very reluctantly she followed Donny out of the poker room and back into the room with the slot machines. She pulled him aside and said, "Look, Donny. You made $7,000 out of $500 without blinking an eye. Why would you stop?" She seemed angry and frustrated. Donny was almost afraid to focus on her thoughts but he did: *I can't believe it. He's got magic in his mind and settles for diddly-squat. Why did I ever think he was so smart? I've gotta' work on him before we come back here.*

Donny wasn't happy about what he'd just heard.

In answer to her question he said, "Look, I stopped because we just made $6,500 in one hour and we're here with fake ID's, and I'm a freakin' mind reader. I don't know about you but that scares the crap out of me. This is about the most I can do in one night...and it's done. And by the way, I don't appreciate you deciding I'm not smart because I didn't stay and risk getting busted or something. This was the smartest thing we could've done." He was happy he got that out. It was the first time he'd stood up to Carla, and it made him nervous to do it.

Carla looked at him, surprised and backed off a little, "Calm down fella', it's just such a breeze for you I want to see you do the best you can." And Donny heard her thinking: *I need to keep him calm. Don't want him throwing a tantrum and deciding not to come back.*

Donny didn't like that either but he didn't say anything. He told himself Carla was being weird because she had too much to drink. He put his arm in hers and they walked back through the casino rooms and left. They were quiet on the way home but it was still early. Carla said, "Why don't you come in and we'll split the profits and … celebrate a little." That was fine with Donny and that's what they did. Her parents were out, as usual, so they went up to her room, counted out $3,250 each, and then they made love to celebrate. Donny went home happy.

Val would be going back to college in a few weeks and she needed some clothes. That day her mom had promised to go to the mall with her, but she didn't feel well and asked if Val would mind if she didn't come. Donny needed new sneakers and said, "I'll go, Val. I've gotta' go to SportsWorld." Val said, "Fine," and, 20 minutes later, they got into her car and drove to Lake Monroe Mall.

The mall wasn't very crowded and that's the way Donny liked it. He split from his sister and went to SportsWorld to get his sneakers, telling her he'd find her in 15 minutes in her favorite department store. He walked through the mall to his store, looked around for a few minutes then saw what he wanted. After he tried on two pairs that didn't fit he found a pair that fit well. He had fun listening to all the "DD time" (daydreaming unimportant thoughts) of random people who were near him. He left the store and walked toward the big department store where Val liked to shop. He was almost there when someone said, "Donny."

He turned around and didn't know who he was seeing at first. Here was this beautiful blond girl who looked very familiar, but he didn't think he knew her. As he walked toward her he searched her thoughts. She was thinking: *Oh Donny, where've you been? I'm so pissed at you for falling for that skank Carla but I still don't think I can help the feelings I have for you. You better notice how different I look.*

"Oh my God," Donny said, "Rose, is ... is that you?" Donny was floored. Rose looked fabulous.

"Of course it is, dummy. Who else would it be? How are you? I haven't seen you for half the summer and now we're almost ready to go back to school."

"Rose," Donny was still in shock, "I can't believe it. You've changed so much. You look fantastic. How did you do this?" He didn't know what else to say.

"I guess I'm just growing up. And, I'm working on it. It wasn't hard you know."

"Well, wow! I am totally impressed. I'm so happy for you." He said. He couldn't help staring at her.

"Thanks, Donny. How've you been? How's Carla?" She asked.

"We're both good, Rose. Jeez, I'm sorry I haven't called lately, it just seems like there's always something going on in my life. But I don't want to lose contact with you. We were good friends, Rose. I need to try a little harder." He meant it. As he was standing there with her, he missed her ... it felt strange somehow. And looking at her new exterior he was amazed he never recognized the potential for her to look so lovely.

"Okay, Donny. But the ball is in your court. You're the one with the girlfriend, for now. If you want to be friends you'll need to call me."

"I will, Rose. I promise. I have to go find Val but I'll call."

"Okay, bye." Rose said and walked off into the mall.

Donny went into the department store and tracked down his sister. She was paying for the things she'd just bought. Donny said, "Val, I just ran into Rose and she has changed so much I didn't even recognize her. Beautiful straight hair, her skin looks different, she's wearing makeup and great clothes … and she's been to the gym. Unbelievable." He said.

Val turned around and said, "Donny, didn't you know that little girls eventually grow up to be women?"

Donny said, "I guess I do now," as they left the store and walked out into the mall.

Things were going well for Sue and me. We were falling in love or maybe already there. We were even talking about the future, you know, beyond high school and college. We talked about careers, family, places we'd like to live. And the more I talked about those things with Sue, the more I grew concerned about what Donny's future would hold.

Donny and I had promised each other we'd have lunch together that week. We hadn't seen much of each other because of the girls. And when we did, we really didn't talk about anything important except some mind reading tricks he'd tell me about. So, that afternoon, sitting in fast food restaurant, I spoke to Donny about the future:

"Listen, Donny, "I started, "what's going on with you and Carla? I mean do you ever do any thinking about your future?"

Donny stared over my shoulder and said, "Not much, Joey. I'm just sort of trying to deal with everything I have right now."

"But, do you even think you and Carla have a future?" I asked.

"I don't know, man. Sometimes I think we're perfect for each other, and then, to be honest, I hear her thinking things that make me feel like she's just using me because I read minds."

"Give me an example of how she's using you?" I said

"Well, you know about the casino. The first time we went we made $6,500 and she didn't want to stop. We just went again two days ago and we won about $11,000. I mean, I'm getting really nervous that the casino managers or someone is gonna suspect we're doing something bad. You know, our ID is phony, so maybe they could take our money if they caught us. It just scares me." Donny was opening up.

"Does she ask you to do other stuff?" I asked.

"Yes, sometimes. She's asked me to be with her when she talks to certain people and tell her what they think. You know, whether they're lying or not. And, she's got this crazy idea about us going on a game show. She says because I can hear everyone's thoughts, we'd be able to know the answers to questions seconds beforehand … stuff like that."

I said, "That's a little crazy isn't it. It sounds like she's just trying to use your ability to help her make money, right?"

"Help US make money is what she would say." Donny corrected, but I could tell he didn't look at it that way.

"Yeah, but still, how do you feel about that?" I asked.

"Actually, that's just the beginning. You talk about the future. Well, when Carla talks about MY future she talks mostly about me being a professional gambler. When I tell her I don't think I could do that she talks about how I could be a top negotiation consultant and hire myself out to companies to help them negotiate important deals. I would, of course, cheat by knowing what the other side is thinking giving me an unfair advantage."

"I don't know, Donny. None of that stuff is good. It's all about gain for her."

"And me," he said very unconvincingly.

"Yeah, and you. But what about using your power for doing good things? I don't know, maybe you could work for the police interrogating witnesses. Or maybe you're a profiler or something for the FBI. Hey, you could make a great Secretary of State, negotiating with foreign leaders. At least you'd be using your powers for the good of your country, right? You could even become the top headhunter in the country, doing job interviews for companies all over. Hell, you'd always know who's telling the truth or what they're lying about."

Donny just shook his head. "Joey, I think Carla will grow out of this. She can be so beautiful and sexy. Maybe she'll change as she gets older."

"Beautiful and sexy doesn't make her a good person, Donny. I've got a sneaking suspicion that when school starts she'll start finding ways for you to help her improve her grades without trying … like reading her teacher's minds, or stealing ideas from the smartest kids in the class. Donny, you've got to be careful."

"I guess so," he said. "But don't worry about me, Joey. I appreciate the concern but I am the one with the power. I'm the one who can read minds, including hers. I know when she's conning me." But he still didn't sound convinced.

Chapter Twelve

It was a common occurrence at the Morris household that summer. Dinnertime found Ed and Susan Morris having dinner with Donny and Val. This was one of the times Val invited Tony to join them.

Tony Donato and his family lived two towns away from Lake Monroe in Fairview, New York. Tony had been living in Syracuse for a while and that's where he met Val Morris. He was a ruggedly good-looking kind of guy and Val fell for him like a ton of bricks. When Donny first met Tony he wondered how he could keep Val interested because, well Donny thought he was kind of dense. Besides, he didn't have a college education. Val was a smart person and Donny couldn't figure out why she was so stuck on Tony until he read her mind a few times. Val and Tony were in a very physical relationship. Like it or not, Val lived for the moments when she could be close to Tony. She didn't even realize that was what the real attraction was. Somehow she deluded herself into thinking she loved Tony for who he was, not what he looked like. But Donny could see it was like a physical addiction and it didn't seem to be going away.

The other thing that bothered Donny about Tony was his family business. His father was Rocco Donato. Mr. Donato was one of those men who've never been convicted of anything but there were always rumors of a Mafia-like organization being covered up by his waste disposal and recycling businesses. In any event Rocco Donato was a scary guy from what Donny had heard of him. And, Tony seemed like he was a miniature, more contemporary, version of his father with a little more culture and social smarts.

Usually, when Tony came to dinner at the Morris' home he was very polite, outwardly caring for Val, and kind of quiet. That night he seemed a little nervous. He was fidgeting in his seat and he wasn't eating much. Val didn't seem to make much of it but Donny noticed.

During the main course of lasagna (Susan Morris had made it because Tony was coming over and she knew he liked it) the family was just talking about things in general.

Ed Morris said, "So Donny, you're going back to school as a senior in just a couple of weeks. We've got to get serious about a college for you."

Donny nodded and said, "Already thinking about it, Dad. We can talk later if you don't mind." Donny thought talking about going to college might make Tony feel a little self-conscious.

Susan Morris said, "That's fine dear. I'll tell you what I've been thinking about … the crime rate in this area. It seems like it's going through the roof. People just aren't safe anymore."

Ed replied, "But I'm not sure that's really true, dear. I think there have been a few high visibility crimes like that murder in Linden, and that scares people for a while … until they catch the guy. Then, it's forgotten."

While no one else at the table probably noticed it, Donny saw Tony stiffen like a board when Ed Morris was speaking. Tony turned white and small beads of sweat broke out on his forehead. Donny was surprised and almost said something. Instead he tuned into Tony's thoughts and heard: *Shit! Why the hell do they have to talk about that? It's done. No one knows. I buried that gun in Martin park so why doesn't everyone just shut-up about it?*

Donny almost fell out of his chair.

Did he get that correctly? What did it mean? He "buried the gun"? What? Was he there? Jesus … did Tony do it?

Donny knew he was turning white too and all of a sudden he was scared. He was scared of Tony. He was scared for Val. He was scared for his family. He told himself to calm down. He needed to figure out what to do.

Donny said, "I'm sorry, I need to use the bathroom. Excuse me." He got up from the table, took a quick look back at Tony, who was still white, and quickly went upstairs to his room.

What had he stumbled upon here? There was just question after question in his mind and they all centered on the fact that Tony apparently had something to do with the murder of that sanitation guy from Linden. Tony's father was in the sanitation business around there and his father has been accused of being a mobster. Tony is in his business. Jesus, is this really happening? Did Tony kill someone for his father? Would Val be dating him if he were capable of that? What if she really doesn't know him? Questions. "Damn" Donny thought, "what the hell can I do about this?"

He sat on his bed for a few moments steadying his thoughts. "There's no way around it. I've got to talk to him and bring up this murder. Then I can see what he's thinking. How do I do this without getting him suspicious or really angry?" Donny knew he had no choice. He had to go back downstairs and talk to Tony before he left.

When he was ready, Donny composed himself and walked back downstairs into the dining room.

Susan Morris said, "You okay, honey?"

"I'm alright, mom, just a little stomach upset." He sat back down at the table.

Val said, "You and Carla eating too much junk I bet."

"Nah, just a little nervous stomach acting up I guess."

Donny knew he had to get into this so he turned to Tony and said, "So Tony, how's the recycling business been these days?"

Tony, whose skin had returned to its normal olive color, said, "Not bad, Donny. People are getting more interested in it. It's the business of the future." Val smiled at him. She smiled at him a lot when he talked.

Donny said, "How 'bout the other family business, you know, refuse collection? Doing okay too? I'm just curious?"

Tony looked like he wasn't particularly happy to be on this subject but he said, "Yeah, people always have to dispose of garbage. We're doing fine." Donny thought to himself that that comment might turn out to have an ironic twist if there was anything to this.

"That's great. Hey, we were just talking about this... Wasn't that guy that got murdered in the sanitation business? Did you guys know him?" He looked directly at Tony.

"There it was," Donny thought, "I laid it out there for him to think about." Then he focused on Tony's thoughts to see what he would get. Tony's face showed signs of extreme discomfort and he thought: *Christ. Why do you have to bring that shit up again? Just shut up and talk about something else.*

Tony replied with a succinct, "No, not really." But Donny didn't want to let up until he got something concrete, either way.

"I wonder what that guy did to get someone angry enough to blow his brains out. I mean, from the article, it almost sounded like some kind of professional hit, you know?" Tony immediately turned red. Even Val seemed to notice.

Donny stopped, focused on Tony and got: *The S.O.B. got what he deserved. He crossed my family and he's gone because of it. I'd do it again in a heartbeat. How can I get this guy to shut-up about this?*

Val said, "Why are we talking about this? So some businessman got shot. There's nothing we can do about it, right?"

Susan Morris said, "You're right, dear. Let's talk about something else."

But Donny had gotten exactly what he was afraid of. Tony - the guy his sister is in love with - shot and killed one of his father's competitors then buried the gun in Martin Park. "Christ," Donny thought, "now what the hell am I going to do? This is going to be a very bad thing for my family and especially for Val. Horrible. Unbelievable!"

Donny started pondering the consequences of the choice he was about to make. He could say nothing. But then Val's very life could be in danger. If he did say something, to whom would he say it? If he told Val she wouldn't believe him. In fact, the police wouldn't believe him either because he didn't have any proof. He couldn't very well go to the police and tell them he knew about a murder because he can read minds. What a mess!

Dinner ended a few minutes later and Donny was almost relieved. But he was so scared for Val he knew he'd have to figure this out quickly, before something else bad happened.

Carla wasn't generally a long-term planner. She liked to live life to its fullest and mostly take one day at a time. But, driving home from the store one night she felt she needed to have a plan for her and Donny because of what could be at stake. She couldn't believe what she had stumbled into with Donny. This could set her up for the rest of her life. She and Donny could make a fortune and never have to worry anymore. And they could do it quickly.

Carla thought, "If I can just get Donny to do a few really big scores we could be done. And then, with or without him, I'll never have to worry about anything again. But, I've got to be careful. He doesn't like to feel pushed. He wants to feel like his power doesn't really matter to me … that I'd love him anyway." She snickered to herself, "Donny-boy has a lot to learn. I could pretty much be with any man I want, can't I? Doesn't he know that? But I've got to be really careful. I must not forget that he can read my mind too. That's the hard part. But, I can do this … and I will."

She went over opportunities they might have to use Donny's power to their advantage. As she listed them out in her mind she would compare them to each other like a market analyst picking stocks for a client. Every time she did it, playing high stakes poker at the casino kept coming up the best bet. The only problem was the phony ID. But that wouldn't last forever either. In less than a year both of them would be 18 and they'd be legal. She didn't think she could wait though. It would be impossible for casino management to figure Donny out, right? How could they prove, or even know, Donny was reading minds? Nope, Carla was convinced the casino route was a rock solid plan. She was going to start working on Donny to get this done … soon.

Donny was driving himself crazy. It was just 24 hours since he discovered Tony's secret and he still was unsure of how he should proceed. He needed help and he decided to call his best friend … me.

He sounded a little shaken when he called and asked me to come over. I was supposed to pick up Sue in an hour but I could stop by Donny's to talk about whatever was on his mind.

When I got to the Morris house Donny was waiting at the door. He looked like he hadn't slept or something and had this dull look in his eyes. I followed him upstairs to his room and he shut the door. He motioned for me to sit in his reading chair and he sat down on the edge of his bed.

"So what's the deal? It sounded important." I started.

"Yeah, it's a big deal. Thanks for coming."

"Did you think I wouldn't? I'm your best friend, Donny. That's what we do." I just wanted to remind him he could tell me anything.

"Joey, this is really heavy. I found out something a day ago that's dangerous and could really rock Val's world."

I said, "I'm listening. What can I do to help?"

"Okay. You know Val's boyfriend, Tony?"

"Sure." I didn't know what else to say about him.

"I think he killed that businessman in Linden … you know, the garbage guy."

I was flabbergasted at the weight of Donny's words, but somehow deep underneath it all I wasn't totally surprised.

"Christ," I said, "how do you know that?"

Donny answered, "I read his mind while were talking about the crime at dinner the other night. He killed the guy and buried the gun in Martin Park."

I didn't know what to say right away. Donny and I looked at each other then looked down to give ourselves time to think.

"Donny, have you ever heard anyone incorrectly? Have you ever misinterpreted what someone was thinking? I mean what if someone was, maybe wishful thinking or fantasizing? How would you know it was just a fantasy?"

"Well, I've thought about that, but I've had this power for over two months now, and here's what I know: I could misinterpret a thought exactly the same way I could misunderstand something spoken out loud. But, there's not a lot to misinterpret when someone says they did it and buried the gun in a specific place." He paused for a second to catch his breath and then he said, "As far as fantasizing or wishful thinking, it would sound the same way as if he were saying it out loud. I'm pretty sure I would just know … just like you would, by the way he said it and how he looked when he was saying, or thinking, it. No, Joey. Tony killed that guy."

I said, "Look, the most important thing here is that this guy is dating Val. I'm sure your first thought was, 'Is she in any danger?' And we can only assume she is. You've got to find a way to get her away from him."

"I know," Donny said, "she's going back to school in two weeks and he spends a lot of time in Syracuse. That's how they met. He used to live there."

"What if you just placed an anonymous call to the police? At least you could tell them the location of the murder weapon. Maybe his fingerprints are still on it or something."

Donny said, "That was my first thought. But Val would probably believe him if he said he didn't do it and, if they let him out on bail, she'd be right there with him. That wouldn't be good enough. Jesus, I can't believe we're even talking about this!"

We were both silent for a minute and then Donny said, "I have no choice, Joey, I've got to tell Val about the whole thing … the Incident, Kwajeh, my powers … everything. Then, once she believes my telepathy, I may be able to convince her she's got to stay away from Tony. I can't think of any other way. Can you?"

"So, let me get this straight. You would do both, right? Call the Police anonymously and make Val understand what you know about Tony?"

Donny said, "Yes. That's about it. I can't think of any other plan that might work."

"Is there something I can do to help," I anxiously asked. I really wanted to help my friend.

"I don't think so Joey. It's been great to have you to talk to about this. You've helped me organize my thoughts and figure out what I have to do. Next step is talking to Val."

We talked for a few more minutes but I knew Donny was anxious to get a hold of Val and try and convince her she was in love with a murderer. Boy I didn't envy him. I wished him luck, told him to call me anytime to talk, and left.

Val was still in her room when I left Donny that morning. It was about 11 a.m. and she may have even been sleeping. Donny tapped on her closed door. No answer. He tapped a little harder, still no answer. He turned the knob and saw Val was in her bed sleeping. He stepped into her room and, in a half whisper asked her if she was awake. She groaned and said, "Sort of. What do you want?"

Donny said, "Val, you and I have to talk. It's very, very important. In fact it's an emergency. If you're getting up I'll wait for you but we need to do this as soon as possible."

Even though she was groggy she caught the disturbing tone in Donny's voice and said, "What is so urgent? Can I shower and get dressed first?"

"Sure," Donny said, "Maybe we can sit outside for awhile. I've got an amazing story to tell you."

"Whatever Donny, I'll be down in 15 minutes, okay?"

"Okay," he said. He closed the door and went back to his room.

Fifteen minutes later he went downstairs to the kitchen. Val was already there drinking tea and waiting for a piece of bread to toast. When the bread popped up she pulled it out of the toaster, covered it with grape jam, and grabbed her cup of tea. "Ready," she said, "This better be good."

She followed Donny outside and they sat in the two chaise lounges furthest away from the house. Val put her plate down on a small table next to her chair and said, "So what's going on? What's so important?"

Donny took a deep breath and started out, "Val, I'm going to tell you an unbelievable story and then I'm going to tell you something else that may hurt and surprise you. Before I do I just want you to know that I'm doing this because you're my sister and I love you. I'd never let anything bad happen to you if I could control it. Know that."

"Pretty dramatic, Donny. I know you love me. I love you too, even though I don't say it very often. Tell me the story." She took a slice of her toast and sat back in the chair.

Donny started with that June day at Kenworth. He told her about meeting Rose and I at the Overlook, the hikes we took, the sun beginning to set and Rose and I leaving. Then came the hard part as he described how he came upon Kwajeh and Mehrak facing the rabid dog near the cliff. He told her about the baseball bat and how he killed the animal. She sat there with her brow furrowed listening intently. She got visibly nervous when Donny described his encounter with the dog. Donny stopped for a second and said, "You with me so far?"

Val said, "This is incredible Donny. Are you pulling my leg here? And why haven't you ever mentioned this before?"

"This is all true, Val … every word of it. But if you want to hear incredible, keep listening. You'll see why I've never mentioned it."

Donny continued with Kwajeh's heart problem, the ride to the hospital, the wait for Kwajeh's exam and then he stopped again. He said, "Okay, Val. Here's where your mind's gonna blow. Please let me finish before you stop me, okay?"

"Alright, go ahead. I'm all ears."

Donny slowly described the scene at Kwajeh's bedside and recalled the translated words that Mehrak uttered on Kwajeh's behalf. When he finished he looked over at Val, and she was holding back a laugh.

"Very funny, Donny. Did you make the whole thing up, or just the last part about the Shaman's gift?"

"Val, I swear to you on my life, your life, and our parent's lives, that every word of what I just told you is true?"

The smile left his sister's face and she said, "So you left the hospital and you could, what, read minds?"

Donny said, "Actually, when I left the hospital I couldn't read minds. The next day I couldn't read minds. But starting the second day I could, well, hear people's thoughts."

Val just looked at him. He tuned her in and got: *This has to be bull, right? No one reads minds. He's always been kind of scary intuitive, maybe a bit more lately, but reading minds?*

"Val, I can tune into anyone I can see ... and hear what they are thinking. I swear, you can test me if you want."

"Test you? Donny, I'm having a lot of trouble believing you but I know you're not lying somehow. I don't know what to make of this."

Donny said, "Test me. Think anything you want. I can tell you what you're thinking."

"Fine," she said. "I'm thinking about a color."

"Red," Donny said.

"Not hard enough. I'm picking a number from one to ten."

"No," Donny said, "too easy. Pick a four digit number, any four digits at all."

"Okay," she said.

"4817," Donny said immediately and Val's jaw dropped.

She said, "You're shitting me here. This can't be. It's some kind of math trick right?"

"No. I'll tell you what, Val. Think of anything. Any thought at all that comes into your head. I'll tell you what it is."

"That's impossible, Donny. Give me a second and tell me what I'm thinking."

Val thought about her friend Marsha and the outrageous price she paid for a pants suit a few days ago.

Donny said, "So Marsha paid too much for a pants suit a few days ago?" He laughed.

Val put her hand to her mouth and her eyes almost popped out of their sockets.

"Jesus Christ, Donny. That is incredible ... just incredible. It's real.

You can actually read minds. I can't believe this happened to you. You did a really good thing and got the most amazing reward anyone could dream of. Wow!" She stopped and thought for a second. She looked a little nervous before she spoke, "But why are you telling me this now?"

Donny sighed. He looked her in the eye and said, "Look, Val. I didn't say anything because I didn't want the world to know. Who would even come near me if they knew I could read their mind?" He decided to tell her only that I knew about all this. He didn't think he should mention Carla. Then he said, "Val, this is going to be very hard to hear, but I'm very concerned and worried about you."

"Me?" She said, shocked. "What about me? What are you trying to tell me? C'mon Donny."

"Okay, Val, here goes. Remember at dinner the other night mom brought up the murder of that guy in Linden?"

"Oh yeah, the night Tony was over. So?"

"Well … uh … I heard something at the table that scared the crap out of me. I listened to Tony's thoughts for a minute because he turned white when we were talking about it. Val, Tony killed that guy and buried the gun. It was as clear as day in his mind. It's why he…

"Oh Christ, Donny. What the hell are you talking about? Tony murdered someone? My Tony? You know I've probably heard enough about your mind reading bull. How can you say something like that? What's wrong with you? She got up and started to walk inside.

Donny said, "Val, wait. This is really, really important and could be very dangerous. Please sit down. I haven't finished. Please," he begged.

Val had begun to cry but she wasn't sure why. She couldn't allow herself to believe her brother had read her boyfriend's mind and discovered he murdered someone. But, in a more rational moment, she recognized that he did indeed read her mind. He heard her think things that would have been impossible for him to guess. Impossible. So what was going on here? She stopped, turned around, and sat back down.

"Donny, you must have made some kind of mistake. Tony wouldn't, he couldn't, murder anyone." Val said.

"Listen, Val. This may be a life or death situation and, it could even be your life. Hear me out. Tony's father has been accused by reputable people of being a mobster. He's in the sanitation business, the same business the guy who was murdered was in. They had to be competitors. I clearly heard Tony think to himself that he murdered the man and he specifically buried the gun in Martin Park. It was all clear as a bell. He thought to himself that he'd do it again. Don't be mad at me . . . I'm just the messenger here. But, Val, Tony is a murderer, a dangerous man. Your life could easily be in danger and if he thinks that you, or I, know about this, well who knows what he might do. You've got to think about who he really may be. How long have you known him? How well do you know him? Have you noticed anything suspicious or different about his behavior lately? Val, ask yourself these questions. Whatever you do, though, you can't, you must not, say anything at all to him." Donny stopped because the tears were rolling down his sister's cheeks.

Val took a deep breath and said, "Donny, he got a phone call last week here at the house. It was from some guy named Louie. My God, Donny, he said they had a special project for him ... that he was getting a promotion and more money. He talked about our future. Jesus, could he really have killed that guy?" Val was a mess but she was a smart lady and the pieces were coming together in her mind. She was beginning to believe that this guy she loved murdered someone ... and it really hurt her.

Donny said, "Val, I want to tell you what I think should happen now. Just listen. I can't go to the police and tell them I read minds and I heard Tony Donato admit to a crime - there's no way in hell they'd believe me. And even if they did, then, everyone in the world would know about my telepathy. What I want to do is make an anonymous call to the police, tell them Tony did the murder, and let them know he buried the gun in Martin Park. They'll most probably investigate that like any other lead. Hopefully there'll be fingerprints or other evidence there linking Tony to the murder. If they haven't already, they'll probably check the link between Tony and his father and the guy from Linden because of their common business interests. And, with Tony as a suspect maybe other witnesses will come forward. I don't know, Val, but we can't just leave him out there, and you can't see him anymore. Does that make sense to you?"

Val took it all in and said, "Donny, I don't know. I need a little time to think about all of this. It's a lot to swallow. I'm going for a ride to be alone and think. I won't talk to Tony. I need to figure this out." She leaned over and hugged Donny, "Donny, I know you're looking out for me. Thank you … I really appreciate what you're trying to do." She got up and walked inside. As Donny sat alone in the yard he just hoped she would make the right decision.

Carla and Donny were going out to dinner. Donny wasn't in a very good mood because of his revelations about Tony and his concern for Val, but he didn't think anything would be accomplished by telling Carla about it. And Carla seemed to be in a good mood. She wanted to go out to a good restaurant partly because she thought they could afford to.

Donny picked her up and they drove to The Chop House, one of the better steak houses in town. Carla was dressed-up and Donny was wearing a newly acquired sport jacket. Donny told himself he was going to have a good time and try and forget the Tony issue for the evening.

They were seated and looking at their menus when Carla said, "Donny, I've been thinking, maybe it's time to go back to the casino for a bigger hit."

Donny got nervous at that prospect. "What's the hurry? And what do you mean a bigger hit?" He asked.

"There's really not much of a hurry except we're going back to school soon and we'll have homework and all the other stuff. It'll be harder to sneak away and go play in the casino. And, you know perfectly well what a big hit is. It's tens of thousands of dollars that will make it so we don't have to worry about money." Donny scanned her mind and got: *He's got to understand how important this is. This money could last us a long, long time. It needs to be really big.*

"Carla, you know it scares me a little to go there with fake ID and use my magic to win other people's money. Doesn't that ever bother you?"

"Look Donny, we've been through this. You need to stop acting like a wimp and take advantage of the gift you were given. You have the ability to win practically every hand at poker. You could make it so we're set for life. Don't you want to be with me for more than just our senior year? Don't you want to feel secure and not have to ever worry about money again? Don't you want to have nice things … and to buy me nice things?" She stopped, wondering if she made her point.

"I'm not acting like a wimp. I'm just concerned. Of course I want to be with you. And I want you to have nice things and security. I just think, well, I think it's a lot to ask. I'm the one who would be taking the risk, right?"

"I'd be right there with you, wouldn't I?" She said curtly.

"Yeah, but I'm not sure it's the same thing," Donny said.

"Well I think we should go there one more time before school starts, make a pot full of money, and never look back. We need to do it in the next couple of days - maybe tomorrow or the next day. Let's just do it, Donny," she said firmly.

Donny thought about it. It really made him more nervous, as he was already nervous to begin with. He didn't know if he could take the pressure. He had this bad feeling that Carla might leave him if he didn't give her what she wanted. It was such a simple thing to her, but she was getting half the money and doing nothing. He knew she was taking advantage of him but, in his mind, it was just the way she was.

"Let me think about it Carla. We can decide tomorrow, okay?"

Carla said, "I don't know why you're having such a problem with this. Nobody else will ever have an opportunity like this and you're afraid to take advantage of it. I don't know, Donny. Maybe you're not who I thought you were."

There was no need to read Carla's mind at that point. She was very clear about what she was thinking. It was up to him. He could do it and make her happy or, he could chicken out and maybe lose her. He didn't like being in that spot.

"I hear you Carla. I just want to sleep on it. We'll talk about it tomorrow."

Donny changed the subject but for the rest of the night he didn't get much from Carla other than one or two word answers and shoulder shrugs. When he dropped her off at her house he kissed cold lips before she said good-night and walked inside. In the car he'd read her thoughts and heard her wondering to herself if he was going to step up and do this or not. She wasn't happy about it.

Chapter Thirteen

The next morning Val was knocking on Donny's door at 7:30 a.m. It woke him up. He looked at the clock and said, "Who's there?"

The door pushed open and Val said, "It's me. I tossed and turned the whole night. I want to talk to you about this." She was holding the morning newspaper in her hand.

"Okay," he said. "Can I take a quick shower and get dressed first?"

She said, "Yeah, mom and dad both left early today so we can talk in the kitchen."

Donny was tired. He didn't even think to read her mind, but he knew it was going to be important. She'd probably made up her mind about Tony.

He jumped in the shower and got dressed. When he walked downstairs to the kitchen Val was there drinking a cup of coffee.

"Did you eat anything," Donny said, concerned.

"I can't eat. Look at this," she said, holding up the newspaper.

"What?" He asked.

She said, "There's a follow-up article about the murder of David Finn. It says that a new witness, from down the street, was able to provide a partial license plate number. I wonder if it's Tony's, Donny. God!"

"Okay Val, I know you've been thinking about this. Tell me what you want to do?"

Tears were rolling down her cheek as she said, "I thought I loved the guy, Donny. I really did. He's good looking, caring, good to me … all those things. I thought I really had feelings for him. I can't believe I fell for a gangster! I mean, that's what he is, isn't he? He's a gangster like his father. And he took someone's life. My God ... how could I have been so stupid?"

"Val ... please ... he's a charming guy. How could you know? It could have happened to anyone. But now, you have to be careful because he's going to want to talk to you. We have to decide what to do . . . NOW! We can't wait anymore."

Val picked up a napkin and wiped her cheeks. She shook her head for a second and said, "Donny, would you do it? Would you call the police? You could call from a pay phone and maybe disguise your voice or something. Tell them about Tony. Tell them where the gun is. Let's hope that piece of the license plate belongs to Tony too. I want them to get him and lock him up forever. I don't ever want to see him again, he scares the crap out of me."

Donny was relieved. He was happy that Val was making the right decision. He'd thought there was a chance that she wouldn't believe the whole thing and that Tony would talk her into siding with him. Maybe he even would have tried to get her to run away somewhere with him. Donny was relieved ... that wouldn't happen.

"Okay, Val, I'm gonna do it in a little while, this morning. The sooner the better, right? I'll call from the pay phone in front of the bus station. I'll tell them I know Tony Donato and I overheard him admit to murdering David Finn and burying the gun in Martin Park. That's all they should need so I'll just hang up. It'll be fine. The only thing you have to do is make excuses for now if Tony wants to see you or talk to you. You don't want to arouse his suspicion or anything but ... maybe you should just tell him you're pretty sick or something. Okay?"

"Okay Donny. Thank you, thank you so much." She threw her arms around her brother and hugged him for a long time.

When she went upstairs Donny had a piece of toast and a glass of orange juice then went back to his room. He gathered all the change he could find and went back downstairs. Val hadn't come out of her room so he just left.

Donny drove to the bus station and parked his car. For whatever reason he felt like a criminal ... like he was doing something wrong. But inside he knew he was doing something right. He put the money in the slot, dialed the Linden police, put his sleeve over the phone to mute his voice, and started talking. He asked for a detective in charge of the David Finn murder. When he was sure he was talking to the right cop he briefly and clearly told him what he knew. Then he hung up.

Donny sat in his car for a few minutes. He noticed he was breathing heavily. This was an emotional thing for him but he knew it was the right thing to do. He drove home and told Val. She cried.

Carla won again. Donny was going with her to the casino to try and win thousands of dollars. She'd pretty much scared him into thinking he'd lose her if he didn't go. So there they were at the Cuyoga Casino valet handing over the keys to Donny's Buick. As they walked inside Donny told himself that he was pretty stupid to do this for a woman, especially a self-centered woman like Carla. But he was still crazy about her and couldn't handle the thought of losing her. He didn't feel like he had a choice.

Donny didn't want to diddle around with slot machines or the roulette tables tonight. He was there on business and he wanted to get it done and get out of there. He told Carla they should head right for the poker tables. They walked through all the rooms to the back of the Casino where he found what he was looking for ... a high-stakes Texas Holdem' game at a no limit table with two empty seats.

He and Carla watched for a while and Carla ordered some drinks. Carla liked to drink, especially for free. After a few hands Donny sat down and bought $2,500 worth of chips, which was basically everything they brought with them. The group of people here seemed a bit more serious and experienced than the folks at the lower limit tables. After a few hands, Donny knew that, if he did not have the ability to read minds, he would not be able to tell when a few of these people were bluffing. They almost seemed like pros. Maybe they were ... it didn't matter. Donny practiced hearing their thoughts and there were no problems.

He thought it would be best to lose a few hands first ... so he did. He also folded early once or twice so no one got the impression he was doing anything funny with the cards. He decided he wanted to wait for one, or a couple, big bluffs when players went all-in with their chips and the pots would be huge. Of course, with aptly timed analysis of their thoughts, Donny knew exactly what was in each player's hand, every hand. He would just focus on each person's mind as each of their cards was dealt. The second they looked at their down cards he knew what they had. There were six other players so it wasn't hard to remember what was in each one's hand. In fact he only remembered the good hands. He purged the garbage hands from his memory and immediately would know if that person was bluffing.

Over the course of an hour or so he was doing well. Carla, who was standing behind him as usual, was keeping mental track of how much they had as soon as Donny put them into stacks. Carla did a visual check and discovered Donny now had over $44,000 in chips in front of him. She had goose bumps.

The table, and Donny's play, had attracted some spectators. There were a few people who were simply into seeing the money move and there were some others. Donny didn't notice the very tall black man with the mustache who kept coming by, looking at the dealer, and then moving on. Nor did he see the fireplug of a Native American man who was only about 5' 8" tall but built like a stone wall. That guy was looking in at the game from behind a player a few chairs down from Donny.

Donny was waiting for his big hand. It surprised him a little when he found himself getting off a bit on the winning. This was new to him. He'd never played at a real casino before this summer and he'd never even imagined having this kind of money in front of him. He knew he had over $40,000 and he thought about quitting more than once. But Carla's hands on his shoulders and neck were all it took to keep reading minds and winning money. He was excited, he was still waiting for the big hand ... the one where one of the players with a lot of chips would try and bluff him on a big pot. He didn't have to wait long.

The gentleman with the black shirt and sunglasses had just sat in a few hands ago. He had a lot of chips on the table and Donny assumed he was looking for big action. Donny thought it was cool that he could even see himself in anything he'd call big action, but there he was. He watched, and listened, carefully as the man made big bets with two and then three, spades showing on the table with only the river card left to be dealt. All the other players folded. This started to remind him of the game he'd played with Rob, when Carla was watching, and he knew Rob was bluffing. The dealer dealt the last card and it was a fourth spade. He heard the other player thinking to himself: *I've got two pair but he ain't got shit or he would've been betting ... and he'll think I've got a flush. I'll see what he does and then raise the crap out of him. Be cool.*

Donny had a pair of eights in his hand and there was a third eight on the table - three eights beats two pair. "I've got him" Donny thought. "He's gonna try and make me think he's got the flush and he'll feel backed up because he's got his two pair. I'll make a small bet and let him raise me through the roof. Then I'll clobber him."

Donny bet a few hundred dollars and the guy in black snickered at him. He started counting his chips and put $15,000 into the pot. Donny called him and raised him $10,000. Donny was as cool as a cucumber. The other player came back with another $10,000 on top of Donny's bet. Donny was ready. He pushed all of his remaining chips into the middle of the table and said, "All-in." The guy with the sunglasses was already way into this pot and he thought Donny was bluffing so he called him. Donny turned over his pair of eights which he added to the third eight on the table and the guy in black threw his cards across the table toward the dealer, got up, and walked out without saying another word.

Carla did some quick estimating and she counted something less than $100,000 total for them. She leaned over and kissed Donny on the lips and hugged him. He was piling his chips up to cash out. He was done and he was very relieved he could go. He turned around to Carla and saw two men standing on either side of her ... looking straight at him.

Mike Freeman was head of security for the Cuyoga Casino. He was a scary-looking man: about 6'6" tall, mustache, totally bald, African American. His assistant was a Native American named Tom Whitefeather who was equally scary with his cast iron body, huge shoulders and arms, hair cut into a short Mohawk, and faded, but nasty, scar on his cheek. Both were dressed in suits and ties, and as they flanked Carla she felt the blood run to her head.

"Give him his money," Freeman said to the dealer. Then he turned to Donny and he said, "Can we talk for a moment, sir?" And he faced Carla and said, "Would you join us too please, ma'am?"

The dealer gave Donny a pile of bills and a drawstring bag with the casino logo to carry it in. As Donny got up from the table Tom Whitefeather took his arm. Donny felt weak in the knees as the four of them walked out of the room and through the Casino toward the front of the building. Donny finally said, "Who are you and what do you want with us?"

Mike Freeman said, "My name is Mike Freeman, I'm the head of security for the Casino. This is my assistant, Tom Whitefeather. We just have a couple of routine questions."

Carla found some arrogance somewhere down deep and said, "Where the hell are you taking us? We haven't done anything wrong."

"Didn't say you did," came Freeman's answer. "We'll talk."

They had almost reached the slot machines up front when, instead of walking to the front door, Freeman hung a left down a hallway. All the doors were closed and unlabeled. Donny got even more nervous. As they continued down the long hallway Donny could feel Carla getting angrier. She wanted to take her money and leave. He hoped she wouldn't say anything stupid.

At the end of the hall Mike Freeman unlocked the door to a small room with a table and four chairs. There were exposed pipes along the ceiling and very little light coming from two lamps standing on the linoleum floor. The chairs were wooden with no cushions or back support. It seemed they were meant to be uncomfortable.

Donny was scared. He tried to read Mike Freeman's thoughts while they were walking. All he got was DD time.

Mike ushered them to two chairs at the back of the table. Tom Whitefeather stood between them with his arms folded across his chest. He looked like a statue to Donny.

After Donny and Carla were in their seats Mike sat on the side of the table. He towered over them and he was a little too close for Donny's liking.

Carla said, "What the hell is this? You've got no right to keep us here. This is kidnapping and don't think I won't report you."

"You do that, miss." He had stopped calling her ma'am. "But first we need to talk."

"What do you want?" Carla said.

"First … you just won a lot of money from my casino. I want to be sure it was on the up and up. We don't like people who cheat for example."

"Are you calling us cheaters?" Carla said. "I'd like to see you prove that we've done anything illegal." Carla's jaw stuck out.

"I didn't say you did. But my dealer says you knew a little too much about everyone else's hands. He said it almost looked like the cards were marked, which of course they weren't but maybe you were doing something else you shouldn't have, huh?" He paused, and then said, "Let me have your ID's please." He reached out his hand.

Donny said, "What do you need our ID's for? Your guys at the front door already checked them. Can't you just ask us your questions and let us go?" Donny searched Freeman's mind for a reaction and got: *Okay … something's fishy with these kids. They're too uptight about their ID's. I'll have Tom run them.*

"Oh shit," Donny thought to himself. "Could they find out they're fake? They're supposed to be the best fake ID's you can buy."

Carla said, "No! I don't have to give you my ID. Your guy already looked at it."

Mike said, "Don't be foolish young lady. Give me your ID now. I don't want to hurt you."

Donny sat upright and pulled the bag of money toward his stomach. What was this about hurting us?

Carla said, "You wouldn't dare harm a hair on my head. Like I said, I'll report you."

Mike nodded at Tom Whitefeather who reached down with one hand, in the blink of an eye, and pulled Carla's purse out from under her arm before she knew what happened.

"Hey," Carla screamed, "you can't do that." She stood up.

Mike said, "Sit down … and shut up, now!" Carla sat but gave Mike an icy stare. Mike turned Carla's purse upside down on the table, pulled her wallet out of the pile, and picked out the Driver's license. Carla was fuming.

"Now yours," he said to Donny. Donny reached into his pocket for his wallet and pulled out the fake driver's license.

Freeman grabbed it and gave it to Tom who promptly left the room.

Donny said, "Hey, where's he going with our ID?"

"He'll be back in a minute." Mike started to walk around the table.

He said, "You are Don Morris and the young lady is Carla Banes. You've been here before. You always win don't you?"

"I don't know, I've had some luck here." Donny said, becoming even more uncomfortable.

"So, do you have some kind of system, Don? Are you using some kind of electronic surveillance equipment? We can search you … take your clothes apart if we need to. Or, are you working with someone else in the casino who's giving you signals? I've seen all of that crap. Eventually you get caught." Mike was glaring at Donny.

Donny said, "No, absolutely not. I'm just lucky. You can search me if you want. I don't care. There's nothing to find. And, and we don't know anyone else in the casino. There are no signals, no gimmicks, no nothing. I swear." Donny was getting a little whiny. Carla didn't like the way he sounded.

Mike said, "We'll figure it out Don. The dealer at your table is one of our most experienced guys. He didn't know exactly how you were doing it but he knew you were getting information about other player's cards. You're gonna tell me, Don."

Soon, the door opened, Tom Whitefeather walked back into the room, handed the ID's and some sheets of paper to Mike and whispered into his ear for a minute. Mike's eyebrows rose as he looked at the sheet of paper. A big grin took over his face and the furrowing in his brow melted away.

"Okay kids; let's see … very little escapes our intelligence reports. Donald Morris, you are a student going into your senior year at Lake Monroe High School, and most interestingly you are 17-years-old." He stopped, looked down at the other sheet of paper and looked into Carla's eyes. "Carla

Banes, you too, are a student going into your senior year at Lake Monroe High School. You are also 17-years-old. Both of you are minors."

He rested his chin on his hand for a second, and said, "It is illegal for minors to gamble in the state of New York. It is illegal for minors to drink in the state of New York. It is illegal for you to have forged, phony driver's licenses in the state of New York." He stopped and looked at them for a second to let them digest the legal implications.

Donny and Carla just looked at each other. Donny had a desperate look in his eyes and he felt a little nauseous. Carla just looked angry. Donny tuned into Freeman's thoughts and heard: *Gotcha' you little shits. I don't know how you did it but the money's coming back.*

Donny's heart sank.

"Guess what, kids? I can have you arrested and you probably will do jail time. How's that sound?"

Donny was shaking. He said, "Look, sir, I'm sorry about the fake ID. A lot of kids get it to buy beer and stuff. Can't we make some kind of deal here? We don't want to go to jail. Please?"

"Yeah," Mike said, "we can make a deal. Here it is. First, hand me that sack of money." He reached out his hand.

Carla said, "No, damn it! We won that money. It's ours."

Mike replied, "Oh? What do you mean 'we'? What exactly did you do to win the money?"

"Um, moral support is all. Donny relies on me for motivation," she mumbled.

"I see," Mike said, "Give me the money … Don-ny." He was making fun of them.

Donny said, "Hold on a minute. There's $2,500 of our money in there. That's the money we started with. It's ours. It has nothing to do with you. It's not your money."

Mike looked at him and moved closer, until his face was six inches away from Donny's. "Don, you're going to learn that many things in life are not fair. If you do bad things, bad things happen to you. Give me the money - all of it. That's the first part of the deal. The second part is if you or your girlfriend is EVER seen on these grounds again you will be in a world of hurt … before you're arrested. Know that I will send your names and photos around to every casino on our national network. You won't be welcome anywhere … even when you're of legal age. And the last part of the deal is the good part for you … I'm not going to send you to jail. You're going to leave the premises and never tell anyone about the illegal events you initiated this evening. Is that clear to both of you?"

Carla and Donny looked at each other. The arrogant posture was gone. They were busted, defeated.

Donny handed over the sack but gave it one last try, "Please can we have our own money back …keep half for your trouble if you have to. We need that money."

Mike took the bag and said, "Goodbye kids. Remember … I NEVER want to see you or hear about you again. Tom will show you out."

Carla was almost in tears. She'd lost her money and her spirit was broken. Donny's magic couldn't get them out of this one.

Tom Whitefeather opened the door and nodded. Donny and Carla got up and followed him out and through the front door to the valet.

Just as Tom was leaving Donny said, "Hey, we don't even have any money to tip the valet for parking our car. Can you at least give us a few dollars for him?"

Tom looked at him with eyes of stone, then smiled for a second and walked back inside.

When the valet brought the car Carla and Donny got in and shut the door. Through the window Donny could see the valet holding his hand out, palm up, in a gesture mocking the fact that he didn't tip him. Donny shrugged his shoulders and they drove away. It was the last time either of them was ever there.

Chapter Fourteen

Donny and Carla didn't talk much on the way home. They were broke, embarrassed, emotionally drained, and angry. For whatever reason, Carla somehow resented Donny's relatively easy acquiescence to Mike Freeman's demands. Donny felt badly about it but what could he do? He dropped her off and told her he'd call her the next day. Then he drove home, went to his room, and fell immediately asleep.

The next morning he was awakened by the sound of his mother shouting in the hallway, "Oh my God, Val ... Val, come see this on TV."

Val yelled back from her room, "What are you yelling about, mom?"

"It's Tony, Val. It's Tony and he's been taken in by the police for questioning."

Donny immediately perked up, popped out of bed and pulled on his pants. He opened the door and said, "What are they saying, mom?" He ran down the hallway to his parents' bedroom where his mother had the TV on. Val had just run into the room. The TV news reporter said that Mr. Tony Donato, son of alleged mobster Rocco Donato, had been taken into custody in connection with the murder of David Finn. They didn't say he was under arrest. The police did come and remove him from his business office in front of his employees.

Susan Morris ran to Val, put her arms around her daughter, and said, "I don't know why they think Tony had something to do with that horrible shooting, Val, but I'm sure they'll get to the bottom of it and realize it's a mistake."

Val hugged her and said, "Mom, I'm not so sure. I feel like a real moron here but I actually think its possible Tony may have been involved. He's been acting funny, talking to strange people, and when that topic comes up he turns white. That guy, Finn was his father's biggest competitor. As much as I thought I loved Tony, I'm beginning to think I was conned and could not see what was really happening."

Her mother looked at her with surprise and said, "God Val, how long have you suspected this?"

"Just a few days, mom, but I'm pretty sure there's something there."

"Has he tried to call you?"

"Yes, I actually talked to him yesterday and told him I had a horrible stomach flu and didn't feel like talking or moving. I said I just had to stay in bed and I'd talk to him in a day or two. Now, if they let him out, he may reach out to me. I'm a little scared of him, mom. I mean, if he really murdered someone I don't want to go near him."

Donny said, "We wouldn't let you, Val. Let's watch this and see what they report on TV and in the papers. We won't let you do anything that would put you in danger."

"That's exactly right, honey. Your family will keep an eye on you. And if you don't want to go back to school right away, I'm sure you can take a few days off. We can just call your advisor. I know they'd understand. But, let's see what happens. What a horrible thing!"

Donny actually felt better. He felt Val would be safe if she stayed away from Tony and hoped they'd have enough to keep him locked up. They didn't generally grant bail in this kind of homicide case either ... once they place him under arrest. "We'll see," Donny thought to himself as the phone began to ring.

When he picked it up Carla said, "Morning Donny. Have you given last night some thought, yet?"

"Given it some thought? Are you kidding? It almost killed me. I don't want to think about it anymore. We both almost went to jail. What else is there to think about?"

Carla said, "We need to figure out what we did wrong, Donny, so we can fix it for next time."

Donny couldn't believe what he was hearing, "Next time? Next time?

Are you nuts? How can there be a next time? We're not allowed at any casino in the United States and we're not even 18 yet. What are you talking about?"

Carla started to raise her voice, "Don't tell me you've been given the ability to read minds and you're going to give up on getting something out of it. What kind of a wimp are you?"

Donny backed off. He just couldn't stand up to Carla for long. "I'm not a wimp. There's nothing we can do."

"There's plenty we can do - other fake ID, Canadian casinos, Europe, private gambling parties. Do I have to paint the picture for you?"

Donny had had enough for now so he decided to tell Carla about Tony, "Carla, I've got other problems right now. My sister's boyfriend, you know Tony, was just grabbed by the cops for questioning about that garbage guy's murder in Linden. Val is very upset. She may even be in some kind of danger. I've got to see how she's doing. I'll call you later, okay?"

"Jesus ... okay, talk to you later." Carla hung up.

Val had gone back into her room to lie down and both of Donny's parents had left the house. Donny was lying on his bed with his hands clasped behind his head, staring straight up at the ceiling.

His mind wandered through everything that was going on. Tony and the murder, Val's feelings, Carla and the Casino, Carla and the future, going back to school, picking a college, his gift and all of it's consequences. It felt like there was something missing in his life. He wasn't sure what it was but even with everything that was going on he couldn't help that feeling. He went through all the events in his mind ... and, finally, it just hit him. He needed to talk to Rose. That was it. He missed talking to Rose. "Should I call her?" He thought. "What if she's mad at me for ignoring her for most of the summer? She should be ... I deserve it." He picked up the phone and dialed Rose's number.

"Hello," Rose said into the receiver.

"Hi, Rose, it's Donny. How are you?" He was tentative because he really didn't know what kind of reception he'd get.

There was silence on her end for an uncomfortable few seconds, "Hi Donny. I'm fine. So … what … have you been out of the country or in a coma?"

He knew he had that coming. "I know Rose, I'm really sorry. I guess I just let my priorities get turned upside down. I really miss you."

"Well, at least you're admitting it. I was missing you a lot too. But then I met Adam."

Donny said, "Adam, who's Adam?"

"Adam is Adam Kantrell. He's a freshman at Lake Monroe Community College, and I think he's already madly in love with me."

Donny swallowed and said, "How did you meet him? How long have you been going out?"

"I met him at the beach about three weeks ago. He's a cute guy and he won't leave me alone. I like him."

"Jeez, Rose, you don't even tell Joey and me about this?"

"Oh, Joey knows. We bumped into him and Sue a few days ago at the movies."

Donny didn't know why but this did not make him feel good. Did he just miss Rose? Did he feel slighted because Joey knew about Adam and he didn't? Could he be jealous? No, that couldn't be it, could it? Rose was just a very good friend, wasn't she? All of a sudden Donny was a little confused. He thought of Carla for a moment but that didn't make him feel any better. What was going on?

"Rose, we haven't seen each other in a long time except for two minutes in the mall. Can I come over and, well, we could just talk?"

"When? Now?" Rose asked.

"Yeah, now. Why not? Do you have to be somewhere?" Donny asked.

"Actually, not until later. Okay. Come on over. Bye," she said and she hung up the phone.

Ten minutes later Donny was in his car on his way over to Rose's house. "I'm just going to see my friend, Rose. There's nothing else going on here. Right?" He asked himself. He didn't know.

He had to ring the doorbell three times before Rose opened the door and led him into the living room. No one else appeared to be home.

As Rose turned around to sit down Donny walked over and hugged her. "You look sensational," he said. "I'll be honest. I didn't know all of this was under the old Rose's disguise."

Rose smiled and sat down. "Thanks, Donny but you're not looking too good yourself. You're very pale and you look exhausted. Have you lost some weight?"

Donny cringed. "Yes, I've lost some weight. I've been through a number of emotional moments in the last week or so and I guess I'm really tired."

"You want to talk to me about them?" She asked in her own cute way.

Donny thought for a second about telling about the Incident, his gift, Tony and the murder, the casino disaster. It was so much he decided to just stick to Tony and Val. He didn't want anyone else to know about his power and it would be hard to explain the casino.

"Well I can tell you I'm very upset because the guy Val's been dating may be a murderer."

Rose's mouth opened, "What? Is that a joke or something? You're talking about that guy Tony?"

"Yes Rose, that guy Tony was taken into custody by the police to be questioned about the murder in Linden. Val was just bowled over by this."

"I can imagine, jeez, Donny that's tough."

"Yeah." He just stared off into space for a minute.

Rose said, "How's Carla?"

Donny thought about reading her mind to check her motivation but decided to play it straight and be honest here.

"She's okay, Rose. Okay."

Rose looked at him and knew something was up. She said, "Well that doesn't sound very good, Donny. What's wrong? This is me you're talking to."

Donny hesitated then he said, "Look, Rose, I know you think I'm a moron for going nuts over Carla because of the way she looks. You are right. I've been dating Carla for over two months now and, well, it's not exactly what I thought it would be. In fact, between you and me, sometimes it sucks." "There, I said it," he thought to himself.

"Hey look, every couple has their problems, Donny. Most people find ways to work them out eventually … or, they end it and move on. Either way, you shouldn't have to torture yourself over it."

Donny was looking at her while he was listening. She really was pretty. He couldn't believe how much she had changed her physical appearance, and he wondered if that's why, all of a sudden he felt an attraction that he didn't know was there before. He found himself wanting to touch her but he couldn't do that. She was dating someone and they were just friends, and there was Carla … he was still confused.

"I appreciate that Rose. Tell me what's going on with you and this guy Adam. Is it serious? Do you feel the same way about him as he does about you?" He asked. Now, Donny was prepared to read Rose's thoughts. He just wanted to be sure he got a straight answer here.

Rose said, "Like I said, Adam is nuts about me and, I like him very much. I enjoy my time with him. He makes me feel like a woman, not a little girl. I haven't been with anyone like that before." Donny focused on her thoughts and got: *You never helped me feel like a woman. I wasn't even a girl to you. I was just one of the guys. And then you started dating that witch, Carla. What a disappointment you were.*

Donny said, "Rose, you definitely are a woman. I think the problem was more that I wasn't a man. Joey and I just acted like what we were, high school boys who weren't grown up yet. But I can tell you this; the experiences I've had in the last two months have caused me to do a lot of growing up, and fast. I feel like I've aged several years over this summer. I know you probably don't believe me, Rose, but I feel like I've really grown up."

She looked at him for a minute and thought that he seemed really sincere. But she wondered what else had happened to him to cause such a drastic change in just a few months.

She said, "If that's true I'm really happy for you. Do you think you'll be able to work things out with Carla?"

"I don't know Rose. Up until just recently I thought I would do almost anything to make our relationship work. But, to be honest, and I can't tell you why right now, Carla has really disappointed me. I'm confused and I don't know what to do about it."

Rose thought for a second and said, "Hang in there Donny. You'll know what the right thing to do is. One thing about you is your excellent intuition. It'll come to you when it will … and you'll know exactly what to do."

Donny said, "I know exactly what to do right now. Can I please have another hug?" He reached out for her and she stepped into his arms. He hugged her tight until he felt her hugging back with the same intensity. Something about it, in that moment, felt right to Donny. They hugged for a long time and didn't say anything and when they stopped it was all Donny could do to pull away from her. They talked about nothing important for another hour and he got up to leave. But before he left he made her promise she wouldn't let herself fall in love with Adam just yet. He wouldn't tell her why but he said he thought there were better things in store for her. She laughed and gave him a kiss on the cheek. Donny promised he would call her and see her much more frequently and he left still apologizing for his summer thoughtlessness.

I stopped over Donny's house a couple of days later just to play pool and talk. We went into the rec room and shut the door. He asked me how things were with Sue. I said they were great … because they were. When I asked about Carla he told me the story about being busted at the casino. Then he told me he saw Rose. I already knew they'd taken Tony in for questioning but none of us, not even Val, knew what the outcome was. Tony hadn't called Val again since she'd told him she was sick.

"So what are you going to do about Carla?" I asked Donny.

"I don't know, man, I'm beginning to feel strange about our relationship. I mean I'm not stupid. I know she's using me for my magic but I think she also really cares for me. Problem is she's filled with both good and evil. I don't know which one will win. And I'm not sure I want to stick around to see."

"And then there's Rose," I said. "You should see yourself when you talk about her now. It's becoming obvious that you've got some feelings going there, Donny. You're aware of it, aren't you?"

"I'm confused, Joey. But I will tell you, the other day at Rose's house, when I was hugging her, I never wanted to let go. Why is this happening now?"

"My two cents ... I think you always had feelings for Rose, and obviously she for you. But you were a kid and you just thought they were friend feelings. I think you've both grown up over this summer and I think you've started to add the physical feelings to the ones you already had and, maybe ... who knows? As for Carla, I don't know, man, you sound like you're getting fed up with her crap."

Just then Val came bursting into the room. "Donny, they've charged him! Tony's under arrest for the murder of David Finn. It was just on the news. They said the District Attorney feels he has enough evidence to indict him. The reporter says they've matched the partial plate the witness saw to a car that was rented in Tony's name. Do you believe that? He rented a car for a murder in his own name. And ... they say they have the murder weapon. It's going to happen. They're gonna get Tony for murder."

"Unbelievable," Donny said. Then I added, "I'm sorry you got caught up in all of this, Val. You couldn't have known. What a shame."

Val said, "Thanks, Joey. I'm actually relieved. I can't even imagine what would have happened if he got away with this and I continued my relationship with him ... a murderer! It's giving me the creeps. It's embarrassing."

Donny said, "I know Val. You'll get past it. I just hope he doesn't try to contact you. I don't think you should talk to him under any circumstances. Just stay away."

"That's not a problem, Donny. If he's in jail I'll just go back to school next week and dig into my work. I'm sure with some time it'll be easier."

"That's the way to do it," I said, "just keep moving forward, Val."

She left the room and Donny and I went back to our game.

I said, "Do you believe we go back to school next week? End of August used to be fun. Now we get to sit in classrooms. At least it's our senior year."

Donny was quiet. Though he was glad the Tony problem looked like it would get resolved, he still had to figure out where he was with Carla … and Rose! He wished he had the ability to see the future instead of just being able to read minds.

Chapter Fifteen

The next week passed quickly. Donny and Carla talked every day and saw each other two or three times but their time spent together mainly consisted of Carla pushing Donny to try going to another casino. Carla wasn't about to give up on this meal ticket and she was pretty persuasive. Of course she wasn't beyond using sex to tip Donny in her direction but Donny was changing. He began to see Carla for a manipulator more and more. At the same time he found himself increasingly attracted to Rose and he began to actually believe he might have made a mistake getting involved with Carla in the first place. But, he didn't yet have the nerve to break away from her. And he actually worried that she might still be able to convince him to do something he didn't want to do.

Tony Donato was indicted for first degree murder and held, without bail, in the county jail. He made one attempt to call Val, but when Mrs. Morris answered she told Tony that Val didn't want to talk to him and it would be better if he didn't try to talk to her until his case was settled. Val was convinced Tony would be in jail for most of the rest of his life, and she was glad it was time for her to return to college. She just wanted to start over again with a clean slate. Before she left she had a heartfelt talk with Donny and broke into tears while thanking him for what he did for her. Their bond was cemented forever by the consequences of her choice of boyfriend and Donny's gift for mind reading.

The first day of school found Donny and I in the same gym class. It was a lot of fun listening to Donny spill what everyone was thinking. He had gotten really good at it and was mainly using it to keep himself amused but he'd tell me things people thought once in awhile, especially when they weren't thinking the same thing as they were saying. For example:

John Miller said, "I really hate Joy Faraday. She's such a stuck-up snob." Donny said he heard John think: *How can I get her to pay attention to me. I'd do anything to touch the skin on her cheek.*

Mrs. Lebow, our Assistant Principal said, "I'm very proud that our school's overall state test scores were in the highest percentile we've achieved in 26 years. Thanks for your hard work." But Donny said she was thinking: *These kids are practically illiterate. A pack of lazy, mutant prairie dogs could do better than them. After 26 years we just stink a little less.*

And our Senior Class President Jennifer Worth said, "I've been dating Michael for three years. We're in love and we'll probably be married even before we graduate college." But she was thinking: *I would really like to try making love to a woman...maybe Carol Teisch from biology class. Michael is so rough and hairy.*

Rose came back to school immediately attracting a lot of new attention from the boys. She had changed dramatically and looked like a different person. All of a sudden guys were talking to her, and about her, and asking her out routinely. She was a pretty cool character though. She mostly either laughed at them or was flat out nasty to the people who had treated her badly when she was viewed as a freckle-faced kid. A little revenge felt pretty good. And, in an odd twist of fate, Rose and Carla wound up in the same Spanish class and were assigned to sit two seats away from each other. They were both incredibly uncomfortable and did everything they could to avoid talking to each other.

Luckily, Sue and I were in the same English Literature class and we managed to sit right next to each other. This was gonna be a great senior year for me, at least as far as English Lit. was concerned.

So, all in all, senior year began pretty much like I thought it would. But then, Donny was going to have to make the decision that could change everything for the rest of his life.

When Donny awoke that Saturday morning he was unaware that this day would have consequences he would feel forever. He had been out with Carla the night before and, of course, she was trying to get him to go to Canada to a casino just over the border. She had even paid to replace his fake ID, which was confiscated by Jim Freeman at the Cuyoga Casino. She spent most of the night lecturing Donny on what they would do differently to avoid standing out and getting caught in the Canadian casino. The irony was that she was suggesting they stick to smaller amounts of winnings but go back more often ... and build their profits with less chance of being noticed for a big win. That had been Donny's original plan until Carla pushed him over the top and he began to feel comfortable with the big pots. Donny didn't agree to anything last night but he came close, if only to shut Carla up.

He got out of bed and went to the window. It was a spectacular early September day … sunny and cool right then but it would warm up to the high 60's before the afternoon was over. Donny climbed into the shower and let the hot water relax his muscles. When he stepped out and dried off he thought he heard the phone ringing. He didn't know if his parents were home, and Val was back at college, so he grabbed his robe from the back of the door and ran to the phone to catch it before it stopped ringing. He picked it up and said hello. All he heard was breathing on the other end. "Oh great," he thought to himself, "a breather … a crank call." He waited a second and said into the phone, "If you've got something to say, then say it. I'm hanging up in two seconds."

"Donald?" The voice said in slightly accented tones he recognized, "Is this Donald Morris?"

Donny had only heard one voice in his life that sounded like that. It had to be Mehrak, the man who served as Kwajeh's voice. Donny was startled! "Mehrak?" He half-whispered into the phone.

"That is correct my boy. It is Mehrak. And I am with Kwajeh, who wishes you well."

"Please, wish him well back," Donny said, and he waited nervously for Mehrak to continue.

"Donald, Kwajeh needs to see you today. It is a matter of great importance. He is sure you will agree once it is explained to you. It would be most convenient if we could meet at the park, Kenworth State Park, the place where we first met."

"Today? Now? I don't understand. Is this, uh, an emergency?"

"In a way Donald. Let us just say it is necessary that we talk today … and Kwajeh needs it to be in person. We would like to meet with you at Willow Overlook, the same place we met on that day in June. Can we do it at 1 p.m. please?" It was more of a statement than a question.

Donny said, "Uh, sure, I guess. I don't see why not. 1 p.m. I've got it. Should I bring anything? Anyone?"

"No," Mehrak's voice replied, "Do not bring anything or anyone. Your presence alone will be sufficient. Goodbye, Donald." He hung up.

Donny hung up the phone and tried to decipher what he just heard. They want to meet him at the park to talk to him about … what, the gift? Kwajeh had said he'd be given a few months to enjoy the gift and then he'd have to make a decision. That must be it. Today was decision day. "Okay," Donny thought, "1 p.m. it is." He had four hours.

Donny called me and told me about the phone call. My eyes popped! "Wow," I said, "I wonder what's gonna happen there. I mean didn't they originally tell you that you would have to make a choice of some kind?"

"Yes," Donny said on the phone, "but I don't know for sure what he was talking about. I guess I'll find out. I'm just nervous, you know? This whole thing has been hard enough to believe, and now I have to see them again? I hope there's no problem or anything."

"What do you mean?"

"Well, basically they told me to use this gift for good. And while I've maybe done that once or twice that's not exactly how I've been spending my time."

I said, "True. But they wouldn't do anything bad to you. You saved that guy's life. I'm sure he's still grateful. Any chance I could go to the park with you?"

"No. They were specific about not bringing anything or anyone. I wouldn't want to cross them."

"Okay. Well, I can't wait to hear what this is. Will you call me when you get back?"

"Sure. It'll be late this afternoon. Bye."

"Bye," I said and hung up. But I was just a little worried about my friend. These were some powerful forces he was dealing with and I guessed anything could happen.

Donny thought about calling Carla, but as he was dialing her number he thought, "Why should I tell her about this? I should see what the conversation holds and then I can decide what to tell her." Donny hung up.

A few hours later he got into his car and headed out of Lake Monroe toward Kenworth State Park. Somehow he wished he had told Rose all about the Incident and its complications. Aside from me, he trusted Rose more than anybody. He knew she wouldn't have judged him or criticized him, except to help him. He wondered, again, what he was thinking going off with Carla and totally forgetting about Rose for much of the summer.

The main thought in his head, as he drove toward the park, was that he wasn't proud of himself. He'd been through this before but he couldn't help feeling he really messed up by not using his gift in better ways. And, he also realized that he'd allowed Carla to push him too far with too many things including the Casino situation. He thought, if he could do it over again perhaps he'd have a better understanding of what it was meant to be used for. But, he also knew that it might just be too late. He'd have to wait and see what Kwajeh had to say.

Donny handed the man at the entry gate to the park his money and took the little brochure and map they give you. He drove into the park and realized he had a ways to go to get to the Overlook where he was meeting them. That was okay. He was a little early. He realized that it didn't matter how often he came to the park, he so loved its natural beauty that he knew he'd keep coming back for as long as he could.

He wondered about Kwajeh and Mehrak. Who were they really? Where did they live? What did they do for money? Where did Kwajeh's power come from? How many people know about him? Are there others like him? And so on. Donny knew he would probably never know the answers to those questions. He would never really understand what had happened to him. How did he read people's minds? How was that even possible? He gave up trying to solve the mysteries and decided to focus on the conversation he was going to have with the two men.

As he drove past the Middle Falls he thought about Val, and what she'd been through with Tony. He felt badly for his sister because he knew she thought she'd loved that guy. That situation was really the only thing he could point to and say he'd done something good with his power. He turned a murderer in to the police and saved his sister from possible harm. At least he could feel good about that.

As Donny was pulling up to the Overlook there were a few people taking pictures of the gorge. He didn't, however, see any sign of the men he was coming to meet. He pulled his car into a space in the back of the lot, locked the door and walked over to a secluded spot on the perimeter of the Overlook, where he was pretty sure no one could possibly overhear his conversation. He sat down on a flat boulder … and he waited.

When he saw that his watch said 1:18 he started to get nervous. What if they weren't going to show up? What if something happened to them? This was undoubtedly really important so Donny was praying that they'd be there.

Without any noise or warning a hand touched him lightly on his shoulder. He jumped. As he turned around he saw the hand belonged to Mehrak. Next to Mehrak, leaning on his walking stick, was Kwajeh.

The two of them were dressed similarly to the way they looked the first time he'd seen them. However, instead of full turbans, they each wore a kind of black skull cap. There was no expression on their faces and, once again, Kwajeh was whispering to Mehrak in that strange language.

Mehrak said, "Hello, Donald. We are sorry to be late. It was unavoidable."

"No problem," Donny said. He was nervous and shaking a little.

"Kwajeh wants you to know that he is thankful you could join us today. It is an important day in your life."

Donny shook a little more. He tried to read their minds and noticed that he got absolutely nothing.

"I'm … I'm glad to see you." He turned to Kwajeh and said, "How are you feeling? The last time I saw you, you were in a hospital bed."

Kwajeh seemed to know exactly what Donny said because he didn't need Mehrak to translate. He leaned over and whispered to Mehrak.

"He is fine, Donald. It seems that every once in a great while his physical body has trouble keeping up with his spirit and he has some trouble. But he wants you to know that we left the hospital a few hours after you. Thank you for inquiring."

Donny said, "I'm glad to hear that." Then he stood still and waited to hear why he was asked to meet with them today.

Kwajeh aimed a stream of conversation, in that strange language, at Mehrak who, again, served as translator.

"Donald, once again Kwajeh wishes to express his thanks for your actions on our part, in this park, those months ago. Saving Kwajeh and I from terrible harm was a kind and generous thing to do. Many other people would not have gotten involved." He paused.

"For that reason Kwajeh gave you the power to know the thoughts of others. You have had that gift for several months now and have many opportunities to make use of it." Kwajeh was nodding his head slowly as Mehrak spoke his words. Then he whispered more words into the ear of his friend.

"Kwajeh would like to ask if you remember the suggested purpose for which the power was intended?

Donny nodded and said, "To … to help people and make their lives better."

Mehrak continued, "That is correct, and Kwajeh would like to know if you did, indeed, follow that recommendation."

Kwajeh's eyes were fixed on Donny's and Donny felt something like electricity between Kwajeh and himself. It was unnerving, but he answered, "I … I'm afraid I didn't do as good a job as I could have, sir. I guess I was so caught up in the power of being able to read people's minds that I got a little carried away with myself. I'm sorry. I really am. I can do better if I have the opportunity." Donny was sure something bad would happen here. Kwajeh and Mehrak both had looks on their faces somewhere between disappointment and disdain.

After a few seconds, Kwajeh continued to whisper and Mehrak said, "It is a shame, Donald, that you chose to take that path. Kwajeh firmly believed that you would use your gift for a much higher purpose."

"I'm really sorry," Donny sniveled.

Mehrak said, "Do you recall when Kwajeh originally granted you this power he told you that you would reach a time when you would be given a choice to keep or give up your new power? You were told that if you chose to keep it, it would come at some sacrifice."

"Yes, I remember clearly," Donny said.

Mehrak continued, "Good. It is that time now. You will have a choice to make." Kwajeh spoke more words in Mehrak's ear. This time it went on for a while. Kwajeh had a lot to say to Donny.

"Kwajeh wants you to know that he does not give such gifts lightly. If he did not believe you were an exceptional young man who did a remarkable thing you would never have been granted such a power. But he also wants you to know that you have truly disappointed him. Your use of this most powerful gift was self-serving and selfish. You, almost exclusively, used it for personal gain or entertainment. And, while you are human and a certain amount of joy for the power can be expected, Kwajeh is saddened by the overall choices you have made."

Donny didn't know what to say so he just looked at the ground and listened.

"It is now time for you to make a choice. Your behavior has dictated the level of sacrifice you will be faced with. Had you taken the higher road and used the power for the right reasons, the sacrifice you would have to make to retain the power would have been minimal ... perhaps the devotion of a specified amount of time donating your skills from the power for the betterment of humanity, or some such high-quality pursuit. But, because you have chosen to take the power so lightly, the penalty to retain it will be very severe."

Donny looked at Kwajeh and thought to himself, "What does that mean? Severe?" As he looked directly into Kwajeh's eyes he had a strong feeling that the Shaman was reading his thoughts.

Mehrak said, "Your choice will be to give up the power totally or to retain in for the rest of your life. You will have 24 hours to make the decision. What you need to know is that if you choose to keep the power, your lifetime on this earth will be cut in half."

Donny wasn't sure he heard right. He said, "If I keep the power my lifetime will be cut in half? You mean I'll die after half my life is over … instead of living to a normal age?"

Mehrak answered, "That is correct Donald. If you keep the power you will have unfettered use of it for your whole life. But you will only live half as long as you would have without it. That is the price you will have to pay."

Donny realized that meant that, if he would've lived to 90, if he keeps the power he'll live to 45. If he would've died of a heart attack at 70, he'll only live to 35. "Jesus," he thought to himself, "this is horrible! What the hell should I do?"

Then Mehrak said, "Kwajeh wants you to think through all the consequences before you make your decision. This is why you're being given 24 hours. At the end of that time I will contact you. You will have only this one opportunity to decide. You will simply pick one choice or the other. There will be no debate about it."

Donny said, "Is there anything at all I can do to change this? Isn't there some way I can have more time?"

Kwajeh didn't say anything to Mehrak at all. He just looked at Donny and shook his head no. That was the end of it.

"Goodbye Donald. Kwajeh and I wish you well and we hope you make the right decision for yourself." With that, he held onto Kwajeh's elbow and guided him away. Donny looked down for a second, trying to get a grip on himself before he went home, and when he looked up again, there was no sign of either of them. They were gone.

The drive back home was mostly a blur for Donny. He couldn't believe what had happened in the park. In fact, there were moments when he felt like it didn't happen at all and was just some kind of dream. All he could do was go back and forth in his head about his choices.

"Is it worth 40 years of my life or so to be able to read minds? That would mean I'd live for maybe another 25 years maximum? That's horrible! But, the things I could do in 25 years with unrestricted use of the gift might make my life incredible. Crap! I wonder what would have happened if I'd used the gift the right way. I might have been able to live a full life with all that power, using some part of my time to do the right things. I'm a jerk. I blew it."

He went on and on like that until he got home. He walked into the house and bumped right into his dad, who said, "What's the hurry, Don? What're you up to?"

"No hurry Dad, just trying to do a lot of things at one time. I've got to make a bunch of phone calls," Donny replied.

"Okay son, but slow down and take it easy," his dad said. But Donny got: *A bunch of phone calls huh? This kid uses the phone like it's free. I bet he'd pay attention if I took it out of his allowance.* "Well," Donny thought, "at least as of right now I still have the power." He went up to his room and shut the door.

Donny wanted some help in making this huge decision. He wanted to ask the three people who knew about his power for their opinions. He called me first.

"Hello," I said.

"Hi, it's me. I'm back from the park." Donny said anxiously.

"I was hoping it was you. Well … what happened?"

"I have 24 hours, actually a little less now, to make a choice."

"So?" I said, "What's the choice?"

Donny said, "It's pretty incredible. I can give up the power, and I assume everything will go back to normal. If I choose to keep the power I can have full use of it … but I will only live half as long as I would have without it."

I was in disbelief at the harshness of the terms. "What!! You're kidding me. If you keep the power you give up half your life! No way! That's not fair, is it?"

Donny replied, "Well that's what I thought, but they told me the sacrifice for keeping the power would have been much less severe if I'd used the power for good things, the way they had suggested."

"Well that sucks doesn't it? I mean, how do they calculate half your life?"

"I don't know. They just know stuff like that."

"But doesn't that mean if you would have lived to 90, you'll live to 45. If you would've died from a heart attack at 50 you'll be gone at 25! Christ, that's only about 8 years from now. You have no way of knowing!"

Donny thought for a second and said, "You know, you're right. It could be anything. I could die in a day or two or I could live for decades. Incredible."

There was silence on the phone for almost a minute. Then I said, "So … what do you think you're going to do?"

Donny was pretty upset. The choice was horrible and he really didn't want to be making this decision. He knew he could talk to Carla and Val, because they were the only ones that knew about his power, but he started to think he should somehow also talk to Rose. He started to get depressed.

"I don't know, Joey. I mean, I want to live a full life. But having this kind of power for years when I'm out of school could allow me to do some amazing things, right?"

"I guess so Donny, but would that be worth giving up half your life? Wow. It's no fun being you right now … and to think I was actually jealous."

"Yeah, the grass is always … never mind. Joey, I'll talk to you later. I have to make some other calls."

I said, "Is one of them Rose? Even though you never told her about this, she would give you an honest opinion that only has your best interests in mind. Other than me, I don't think there's anyone that cares more about what happens to you than Rose."

"Maybe, Joey. Thanks. See you later." He hung up the phone.

He sat for a while thinking, and then he picked up the phone and dialed his sister's number at college. He got her answering machine and left a short message asking her to call him and hung up.

Donny decided that the conversation with Carla was too important for the phone and he needed to speak to her in person. He dialed her number and, when he got her, he asked if she'd meet him at a local cafe for a cup of coffee. He didn't want to go to Angelo's because he was afraid of running into people they'd know.

He drove to the cafe, parked in front and walked in. There was almost no one there because it was only about 5 p.m., too early for a dinner crowd. After a few minutes, Carla walked in. She came over to the table, leaned over and kissed Donny lightly on the lips, and sat down. The waitress came over and gave them menus but Donny and Carla both just ordered coffee.

"What's up Donny-boy?" She asked. Donny realized he hated when she called him that.

He said, "Carla, something really big has happened to me and I need to hear what you think about it. As strange as it is, you just have to take my word for everything I'm going to tell you."

Carla started to look worried. She furrowed her brow and said, "What is it? What happened?"

Donny reminded Carla of what the Shaman had said months ago when the Incident had occurred … the part about the day coming when he'd have to make a decision, and maybe a sacrifice. Carla shook her head up and down … she remembered.

Then Donny explained the events of the day: the call, the trip to the park, the decision to be made and the consequences of the choices. During the entire time he was speaking Carla's expression didn't change. She seemed almost hypnotized by his words. When Donny was done he looked up at her and asked, "So, what do you think? What should I do?"

Carla said, "Donny, I think it's pretty clear what you should do, don't you? I mean, you could always choose to do nothing, have nothing and be nothing. You could just do … nothing. And that's what your life will be … what it was going to be in the first place … just like everyone else's … nothing! You are being given the chance to do, not just something, but something incredibly powerful. That old Shaman has given you the power to do whatever you want to do. He has given you the power to read minds, to never be lied to, to always know what's in the other guy's hand, to always know more than anyone else. What an amazing thing that is, Donny. You must know that by now."

He was looking into her eyes and he was a little disturbed by the almost feverish glow that had overtaken them. "I know it's amazing, Carla. But, what good is it if I only live for half my life?"

"Donny, here's the way I see it … very simply. We could seize the power and conquer the world in the forty or however many years you'll have. We could lead a life like no one on this earth ever has. We could accumulate great wealth, do amazing things, and have more fun and money than anyone ever dreams of. Or … you could live twice as long in an everyday, boring life doing nothing special and having nothing special. You'd have to be stupid to throw away that opportunity, no matter how long it lasts, for a few extra years of nothing special." She stopped to see if her words registered with him.

Donny thought about pointing out that much of the reason he did nothing selfless with his power was because he was trying to please her, and all she wanted was more material things that made her happy. He was beginning to emerge from his denial of Carla's selfish motives and admit to himself more clearly that all Carla really cared about … was Carla.

"You know, Carla. I'm not sure what I'm going to do yet but I've got to say I think you're not looking at this with an eye toward what's best for me, or even what's best for anyone else. It's all about what can I do for you, even if I have to die 40 years too early to do it. Isn't that right, Carla?" It felt good to stand up to her.

Carla took a breath and then, "I can't believe what a wimp you're being, Donny. You're going to lay this on me? Was it me who beat Rob and everyone else out of their money in that first card game? Was it me who accepted the fake ID with your name on it? Was I the one playing the hands out to win big bucks at the casino? I don't think so, Donny. You could've said no any time you wanted. But you didn't, did you? You did it and you liked the idea of winning a ton of money just as much as me. And, you know what? You're going to keep winning us money and enjoying it, because you know that for us to stay a couple, that's what we have to do. That's what we need to do. It's the chance of a lifetime. We will be successful and no one will stop us. You want it as much as I do … and you're gonna get it for us. You know you will."

Donny felt like he had been spanked. But while there was some small truth to Carla's words, he knew she was wrong. He was not going to keep winning money for her. He couldn't. Why should he? And what kind of life would he have with Carla in his 20's, 30's and 40's if he even lived that long? She would never have enough. Donny knew he was seeing the truth at last. He tuned into Carla for a moment and got: *Come on Donny-boy, this is no time to grow a backbone. I've got things I want out of life and YOU are going to get them from me. If you die at 40 we'll be so rich by then I'll never have to worry about anything else in my life. Never. No Donny, you can't back out now. The power is ours and we need to keep it.*

Donny hated hearing that. She'd thought "The power is ours." "Ours!" "We!" Donny thought. Unbelievable - she wanted the benefits of the power but no blame for its misuse. Donny was upset by this conversation and wanted to leave. He threw a few dollars on the table, stood up, and said, "Carla, I've gotta' go now. I promised mom I wouldn't be late for dinner."

She said, "Okay, but am I going to see you later?"

He heard himself say, "Not tonight, Carla. I need to be alone and think this all the way through. I'll talk to you tomorrow."

Carla thought, *I need to keep on him so he doesn't blow it*, and Donny read her thoughts.

"If you need to talk, Donny, just call. I'll be home. Maybe you'll just want to come over and cuddle or something," she said with an attempt at a sexy wink. It didn't work … Donny just shook his head and waved as he walked out. He got back into his car and drove home.

When he got home, Donny again went right up to his room to call his sister again. She answered on the first ring.

"Hello," Val said.

"Hi Val, it's Donny. Boy am I glad I got you. Are you doing okay?"

"Yes," she replied, "it's good to be away from there. I've got some healing to do."

"I know. You're a strong lady … you'll be fine. Me, on the other hand, I don't know, I need your opinion here."

"Glad to help sweetie. What's the matter?"

Donny took his time and poured the whole story out into the phone. Val didn't interrupt him even once with questions. He could tell she was amazed.

"So I've got till tomorrow at around 1:30 to make the decision."

Val didn't know what to say at first. But when it all sank in she said, "Donny, you have no choice. You've got to give up the power, right? Could anything be worth sacrificing half your life? Really?"

Donny said, "I don't know, Val. Sometimes I think what I could accomplish in half a lifetime with the ability to read minds might make it worth it. Do you see that?" He asked.

"No. Not really. I can understand why you'd have to think about it but, Donny, you may be talking about giving up 40 years of life. You had better think very carefully about that. It is huge … and it sounds like you're only going to get one chance at this decision. I wish I could help you see this more clearly, Donny."

"Well, thanks Val. I see your point and I really appreciate your concern and your thoughts. Also, I just want you to know I love you Val. I haven't always been the greatest brother but I've always thought of you as special and I'll always do whatever I can to help you find happiness." He was almost in tears.

Val was nervous, "Donny, you're scaring me here. Why are you talking like there's going to be a suicide note on your pillow? I love you too. This will be all right. You WILL figure it out and make the right decision. I know you will. I have to go, Donny, but call later or tomorrow if you want to talk some more. I told you what I would do. I just wish I could make the decision for you. Bye, Donny."

"Bye," he said, and hung up the phone.

It was close to 8 p.m. and the same thoughts kept chasing their tails in Donny's head. In an instant he realized he had to talk to Rose. That thought just stuck out in his mind like a giant billboard in a small alley. He needed to tell Rose about all of this and see what she thought. He needed her.

Donny got up off the bed, picked up the phone and dialed her number. After the 4th ring he was ready to hang up when a very out-of-breath Rose said, "Hello?"

"Rose," Donny said, "I thought you were out. I'm glad I caught you."

"Caught me?" She said, "You almost killed me. I was downstairs doing something and the phone in the living room is broken. So I ran up the stairs, banged my toe on the top step, and stumbled into my room. This better be important ... I've gotta' get going."

"Where are you going, Rose? It's really, really important that I talk to you, in person, tonight ... now."

"What? I've got a date with Adam and I should have been there already. I'm going to meet him at his house and...."

Donny cut her off, "Rose, listen to me. This is a matter of life and death. I'm not kidding. My life is on the line here and I need to talk to you ... very badly."

"Come on Donny. You're just yanking my chain. What am I supposed to tell Adam?"

"Tell him you got sick. Could happen, right?"

"What is so important you can't tell me on the phone, or some other time?"

Donny's voice was sobering, "Rose I'm not kidding here. I'm going to tell you a story you won't believe with an ending that needs your input. Please, I'm begging you. Cancel your date and let me come over."

Rose thought for a second then said, "Alright, Donny. But this better be the real deal. I like Adam and I don't want to blow our relationship on a whim from you. I'll call him but you can't come over here. My parents have company. How about if I come over to your house?" She asked.

"Okay, Rose ... whatever's good. Come on over as soon as you can. Bye."

They both hung up and Donny somehow knew inside this might be the most important conversation of all.

Forty-five minutes later his doorbell rang. He opened it and started to lead Rose up the stairs. She said, "Hey, where are we going? What's wrong with the rec room?"

Donny said, "My dad's in there watching a tape of some old football game. I want to have a private conversation with you. The best place is in my room. C'mon."

"Alright," she said and they went upstairs to his room and closed the door.

Rose sat in his reading chair and Donny sat across from her at the edge of her bed. He took a minute to take her in and, once again, he was smitten by what Rose looked like. Her hair was back in a long ponytail, she had light make-up on and her eyes, as usual, were smiling. She was wearing a silver top that clung to her newly developed shape, tight black jeans, and flip-flops. Donny thought she looked beautiful.

When they were settled Rose kicked her sandals off, folded her legs into a yoga position on the chair and said, "Okay, so what's this all about, Donny? It better be good."

Donny said, "Rose, the things I'm about to tell you will be unbelievable. Sometimes, I don't believe this happened myself. I'm just going to ask that you let me finish describing the first part of it to you without interrupting me. I'll answer all your questions and even give you proof what I'm saying is true when I'm done. Then I'll tell you the second part … which happened today. Okay?"

Rose's eyes were wide open. She had a feeling she was going to hear something huge, so she was bracing herself as she nodded yes.

"Do you remember that Sunday, back in June, when I met you and Joey at Kenworth? We met at Willow Overlook, hiked around for few hours, and then you and Joey left. I got home pretty late that night."

"Yeah, I do. It was a beautiful day," Rose recalled.

"It was a beautiful day … and an amazing day. It changed my life." Donny started recounting the day from the point where he was left sitting on the big boulder. He described the entire Incident, Kwajeh and Mehrak, the rabid dog, the trip to the hospital, and the conversation in Kwajeh's room. He went into as much detail as he could remember when he explained the conversation during which Kwajeh granted the gift. Rose sat looking mesmerized by the whole story. Donny didn't bother to read her thoughts but he sensed a general skepticism as soon as he mentioned the gift. He continued, describing the 48 hours after he got home and the first occurrences of his ability to read minds … with Val.

At that point Rose began just nodding her head slightly from side-to-side as if to say, "Mm-mm-mm, you poor thing. You probably believe all of that too." But she didn't say anything.

Then Donny said, "So that's it … the first part of the story. I've been blessed, or cursed, with that ability since that day. The only person I've found so far whose thoughts I couldn't hear was Kwajeh himself." He looked at Rose for a reaction. All he got was the mild head shaking.

"Rose, say something … please." He begged.

Rose finally said, "What do you expect me to say, Donny. C'mon, why did you really bring me over here? I don't know why you would do this to me. Do you think it's funny?"

"Look, every word I've told you is true - every word. I didn't tell you originally because Joey knew and I felt I had to tell Carla ... because we were seeing each other. I didn't want to get you involved."

"Oh, so now you want me involved? Why? Donny this just sounds like a load of crap. I think I better go, huh?"

"No, Rose, no. Look I've made some major, major mistakes with this whole thing ... and not telling you about it was one of them. But I'll prove it if you want. Test me. Go on ... test me."

"Don't be ridiculous," she said. "You've probably learned some kind of fake magic trick. I don't know ... it sounds silly."

Donny said, "No, I insist. If I focus on your mind I can read your thoughts. So be careful," he laughed. "Seriously, I can tell you anything you are thinking. Just try me. Pick a number."

"Oh Donny, come on. Pick a number from one to ten, multiply it by eight, subtract 4 ... blah, blah. I know it's a trick and I'm not biting."

"No Rose. Pick any number, or a color, or a person, or a place ... or anything at all. Don't even tell me what category it's in. Just think it. I won't ask you anything at all about it. I'll just tell you what it is. Go on."

Donny got: *Okay, dummy, how's 46839?*

He said, "46839." Rose blinked.

"Impressive Donny but still some kind of trick, right?"

"And don't think of me as 'dummy' please," he said. Rose blinked again.

Donny said, "Try something else. Something no one but you knows - anything that would be impossible for me to know."

Rose thought for a second and Donny got: *No way anyone knows that I once punctured one of Drew Burger's tires because he called me a little boy.*

Donny said, "So Drew Burger called you a little boy and you took it out on his tire? Shame on you." Donny said, laughing.

Rose wasn't laughing. Her jaw dropped. "How … how did you do that?"

"I told you I can read minds. It's the truth. One more, Rose, and then I'll tell you the rest of the story."

Rose was absolutely amazed. She had to believe him now. She decided to try one more thing so she thought of Carla and couldn't help thinking how much she disliked her and how selfish she was. She thought Donny was a moron for falling for the pretty face with nothing underneath.

Donny blushed a little then he said, "I know Rose, you hate Carla because she's selfish. And you think I'm a moron for dating her. You just thought 'a pretty face with nothing underneath.'"

"Jesus, Donny. You are scary. This really happened? You were really given mind reading power by a Shaman for saving his life. Wow! You'll never be the same again," she said.

"Maybe, maybe not … there's more to tell." Donny went on to tell Rose about all the significant events related to his mind reading that had taken place that summer. He felt guilty about taking money from Rob and the others in card games. He was proud he could help Val discover the truth about Tony. He saved everything with Carla for last.

As Donny was talking to Rose and staring into her eyes he wondered, again, what on earth had possessed him to go running after Carla. Rose was beautiful on the inside as well as the outside. She was lovely, smart, caring, truthful, faithful and very special. Donny started to recognize that Carla was just a symptom of him being a teenager. The more he searched himself the more he found deep-rooted feelings for Rose. He'd just chosen to ignore them for a while but now that he realized fully that Carla was just a temporary walk down the wrong path, he wondered what he should do about Rose.

Donny told Rose everything about Carla and their relationship. He explained how she pushed him to play cards and tell her things people were thinking that she could use for her own benefit. He told her about the card games, the casino trips, the fake ID, and being busted. The more he listened to himself talk about himself and Carla, the more it made him sick. "How could I let myself do that?" he thought. He knew Rose understood what he went through. What he didn't know was how she felt about it, and about him now.

When he was finished explaining all that to Rose he said, "Now you know almost everything. You need to hear about what happened today … and then I can ask for your help."

Rose was hypnotized. She said, "My help? With that kind of power what on earth would you need my help with?"

"You'll see. This has been an amazing day. This morning I got a phone call from Mehrak asking me to meet with him and Kwajeh back at Kenworth Park, at the Willow Overlook." Rose's mouth dropped open again and her eyes bugged out. Donny went on to explain the day's happenings including the return to the park, the conversation, the choice, and the timing. When he was done, he just looked at her. There was a tear rolling down her cheek.

He grabbed a tissue from his night table and handed it to her. "Why are you crying?" He asked.

She said, "I don't know. I just feel for you. You have a lot on your shoulders and no matter what you do you will really never be the same old Donny that I lo..." When she realized what she was saying her voice just trailed off.

Donny walked over to her and put his arms around her. "What should I do Rose? What would you do?" He asked.

She sniffled a little, blew her nose into the tissue and said, "Donny, you've got to give up the power. I mean, maybe if you hadn't used it so badly, maybe if you'd done big things that changed the world, or even lots of little things that made people's lives better … maybe then you'd have a minimal sacrifice for Kwajeh and you could have kept the power. But now you would lose half your life, Donny … maybe 40 years of living. How could you do that? Don't you want to see your children grow up and have their own children? Don't you want to grow old with the woman you love, the woman you'll marry? Don't you want to see what happens to the world and the people in it? It can't just be about you and your power for 20 years. That's selfish and it's not you. You are a wonderful, sweet, smart guy who deserves to live a full life, to love and be loved by the people you care about. I can't let you make the wrong choice here Donny. I care too much about what happens to you."

Rose grabbed onto him and held him tight. There was electricity between them that Donny had just not felt with Carla. He knew he was falling in love, or maybe he was already in love, with Rose. He knew she genuinely and unselfishly cared for him as he did for her. He didn't want to let go. The two of them began to move in a smooth, swaying motion with their arms around each other. If they had been singing, it would have been perfect harmony. They just rocked back and forth, holding each other. Neither one felt time passing. They were right where they both wanted to be until Rose stepped away to go home.

Donny said, "Rose, I want you to forgive me."

"For what?" She asked, gently.

"For being stupid and not understanding what you and I were. I'm sorry and I will make it up to you … I mean, assuming you want to be there with me." He hesitated briefly and said, "So what about Adam?"

Rose laughed, "What about Adam, Donny? If you've read my mind you already know that I've felt this way about you for years, since we were kids. Adam's a nice guy but he'll get over me. What about Carla?" Rose asked.

"I'll talk to her in the next day or so. She'll be angry because she won't get her way. But she deserves what she gets."

Donny held Rose's hand as they walked downstairs. They walked out the front door to her car. Donny said, "Thanks Rose, it meant so much to me for you to be here tonight. I can't tell you how much." She looked up at him and brought her lips to his. The kissed seemed to go on forever and when it was over Donny felt happy for the first time in months. He told her he'd call her tomorrow as he shut the door to her car and walked back to the house. He was smiling as he went back inside.

Chapter Sixteen

Donny called me at around 11:00 in the morning on Sunday. He asked if I could come over and hang out when he got the call from Kwajeh. I said I wouldn't miss it for the world.

When I got there his parents were at church and he was shooting pool in the rec room. The first thing I did was to ask him how his conversations went the previous day.

"Well, I got hold of Val and she said pretty much what you did … that it's not worth half my life to be able to read minds."

"Did you talk to Carla?" I asked.

Donny told me about their conversation and the way he felt about it. He was really turned off by Carla. It seems he finally saw all the way through her selfishness. God, it took him a long time. He told me he was going to call her later, go see her and end it.

"So, then you'll be a free man, huh?" I said.

"Well, I didn't tell you about my talk with Rose. She came over last night and I told her the whole story, everything, from the beginning."

"Wow! She must have been blown away. How did she react?" I asked.

I didn't expect to see the look I got from him. He turned a shade of pink when he described his newly realized feelings for Rose. He told me what she said and how good it made him feel. He told me about the hugging and about the electricity between them. I understood. I was just waiting for that to happen with them. They should've been together a long time ago but, he had to grow up first.

We shot a few racks of pool and made sandwiches from stuff we found in the refrigerator. At about 1:30 we were back in the rec room. The phone rang. Donny got very nervous as he picked up the receiver.

"Hello," he said.

"Hello Donald, this is Mehrak and I am with Kwajeh. It is time for your decision, yes?"

"I know. This was very hard for me, and I want Kwajeh to know how much I appreciate his giving me this gift to begin with. I can only say I'm very sorry I did not use it wisely. I'm sorry I disappointed him."

"Kwajeh understands, Donald. He knows the frailty of the human mind and how easily one can go astray. How do you choose to proceed?"

"I'm going to give up the power," Donny said. He felt relieved that this would soon be over.

Mehrak said, "You only have one chance to make this decision so you need to be absolutely sure about it. Are you absolutely sure you wish to give up the power?"

Donny said, "Yes I am. I can't imagine giving up half my life for something I've already misused so badly."

"Very well, then. In a short time you will find you no longer have the ability to hear the thoughts of others. Kwajeh, again thanks you for your efforts on our behalf in the park that day, and he hopes that you have taken something of value from this experience. You will not hear from us again, Donald. Goodbye and good luck to you." The call was over.

Donny hung up the phone and looked at me. "It's over," he said. I'll probably lose the power in a little while. They told me they wouldn't contact me again and wished me luck. That's it."

"I think you did the right thing, Donny. Now you can just move ahead with your life the way it was supposed to be. And, still, you've had an experience that no one else you'll ever know can match. You are a lucky guy." I meant it.

Donny said, "I need to talk to Carla ... but what I really want to do is see Rose. I just want to hug her. And I know I love her."

It was good to hear my friend talk like that. He was given ability unrivaled by anyone I'd ever meet. And, almost from the day he got it, he was miserable. This was a very good day.

After I left, Donny called Carla. She wanted to know what his decision was and he said he'd like to talk to her in person. They agreed to meet at a little park near her house.

When Donny pulled up Carla was already sitting on one of the benches looking at a pond. Donny walked over and sat next to her.

"Hi," he said and he tried to read her mind. He got: nothing, nothing at all. It was gone.

"Hi. So what happened?" She asked.

"Well, I thought about everything that's happened this summer and the effect the decision would have on the rest of my life. I told them I was going to give up the power and live a normal life," he said firmly.

Carla stared at him, and a growing look of contempt came across her face. "You didn't? You couldn't be that stupid, could you? Tell me you didn't give up the most powerful gift anyone's ever given anyone else." She practically spat the words.

"I did, Carla, and I'm really glad to be rid of it. It took me a while but I finally realized that I totally misused the gift. It was all about personal gain and not about helping people. It was more about you, and me and not about the rest of the world. I discovered I want to live a good life, Carla. I want to be in love and grow old. I want to have kids and grandkids. I want to make a difference in the world, not just take from it. I was wrong to do some of the things I did. I'm really glad to be done with it." Speaking the words to Carla was definitely cathartic for Donny.

Carla stood up so she could talk down to Donny, "I don't think I've ever seen anyone make a dumber decision. You've given up the greatest gift you ever could have had. Now you will be just like everyone else. You had the world in your hand and you dropped it. Ugh, you're a moron. And I hope you don't think there's any hope for you and I because the last ounce of attractiveness you had was gone the minute you stopped being special."

Donny wasn't upset at all. In fact he smiled at her. He stood up, put his face really close to hers and looked into those beautiful eyes. "You … are the devil, Carla. You are evil and selfish through and through. You think only of yourself and no one else. You have nothing inside you that's good or pure. You are a fraud and I can't imagine what would make anyone feel real love for you. I was blinded by your outer shell and it's a good thing you have it because there is nothing else about you that's even the slightest bit real. Goodbye, Carla. I know you'll find someone you can fool into loving you … until they find out who you really are."

He turned around and walked to his car and Carla yelled something at his back but he didn't hear it. He didn't care. He just wanted to go see Rose. He felt really good inside.

Chapter Seventeen

10 YEARS LATER.....

Looking back now, our senior year at Lake Monroe High was pretty uneventful. I don't believe Donny and Carla ever spoke another word to each other, and he and Rose pretty much became joined at the hip. Sue and I and Donny and Rose had some good times during that year ... like the time we stayed out all night at our senior prom and wound up skinny-dipping and sleeping at the beach until the sun came up. It was a fun time.

Carla started dating Michael Berger that year. He was a big, good-looking, moron who played football and ran track. He also almost didn't graduate because he got a D in English.

After high school, Donny and Rose both went to colleges in upstate NY. They were close enough to be able to see each other on many weekends and, for four years, that's exactly what they did.

Sue and I both went to a big school in Michigan. It was like fate let us get into the same school so we were together just about every day in college. Two weeks after we graduated we were married. Of course, nobody was surprised. When I graduated law school I got a job with Sue's father's law firm in the western New York branch as a trial lawyer. We moved to Buffalo and bought a beautiful home in the suburbs. Then we had twin girls and a son two years later. Also, we adopted a dog from the West Shore Animal Society. Life has been good to our family.

I heard Carla went to a 2-year community college and married an obnoxious guy for his money before she graduated. Sadly for her, he turned out to be abusive. Rumor was she took several beatings before she had him arrested. They say she didn't wind up with much of his money because he apparently found ways to hide it from her attorneys. The last time I heard about her she'd gained a lot of weight, become an alcoholic, and was living at home with her mother. Carla's life seemed to have paid her back.

To this day, Donny and Rose have never left each other's side. They are as much in love as two people could ever be. When they graduated college they decided to spend a couple of years overseas in the Peace Corps. They got married in Lake Monroe and went down to Nicaragua to help build schools and teach underprivileged children. Donny had found the value in service to others and, along with Rose's love, which was enough to help keep him contented and motivated. Eventually they moved back to New York and had a son. Funny thing about that boy - he was such a smart, perceptive kid that people said they could swear that he knew exactly what you were thinking. It was like he could read your mind. Imagine that!

About the Author

Steve Godofsky recently retired from the radio industry after decades of service. He served as Senior Vice-President and Regional Vice-President for the third largest public radio company in the U.S.

Mr. Godofsky has Bachelor of Science and Master of Business Administration degrees with majors in marketing and marketing research.

He has managed more than 20 radio stations in 13 cities, run 3 broadcast companies, and consulted over 40 radio stations on their programming, marketing, sales, and management practices.

The author of articles on radio management and leadership for trade publications, poetry, and fiction, he is currently working on his fourth novel.

He also writes music, sings, and plays keyboard instruments.

Mr. Godofsky was born in Brooklyn, NY in 1947. He now resides in Charlotte, North Carolina with his wife Sandra and his Golden Retriever, Hank.

www.ingramcontent.com/pod-product-compliance
Lightning Source LLC
Chambersburg PA
CBHW070518260626
47161CB00004B/1585